PRAISE FOR

The Plain of Pillars

Independent Publishers GOLD Award, Best in Fantasy.
PenCraft 1st Place in Fiction
National Indie Excellence FINALIST in Fiction.

'*The Plain of Pillars* retells Celtic myths and revitalizes ancient folkloric traditions, weav[ing] a powerful critique ... of colonization, apathy, and individualism. Griffith demonstrates a mastery of genre fiction and mythology, employing narrative techniques that are both lyrically impressive and philosophically engaging.'

– INDEPENDENT BOOK REVIEW

'A captivating retelling of Celtic mythology that will resonate with modern readers...with compelling characters, intriguing dialogue, and evocative descriptions, Griffith keeps this folkloric tale alive and vibrant...the novel itself feels like a form of resistance against colonization and cultural extinction.'

– KIRKUS REVIEWS

'Griffith's wonderful work, *The Plain of Pillars*, transports the reader into ancient Ireland, a misty dream like world through the genesis story of a people who come from the stars, an ancient, Irish story that is strikingly like other ancient narratives that proves to me that we are all indeed related.'

– TAYLOR KEEN, author of *Rediscovering Turtle Island.*

'Shivers across the body, palpitations of emotion, struck by thoughts of awe, captivated by words—this book is felt! Weaving from a space before time, *The Plain of Pillars* is a poetic blueprint for reverence and morality. A great gift for a world in need.'

– DANE SCOTT, indigenous Māori storyteller, Taonga Pūoro musician, and filmmaker.

'An extraordinary book, *The Plain of Pillars* is potent and activating—a stirring, a remembering of ancient bones. Its timing is without a doubt divine.'

– CHELITA KAHUTIANUI-O-TE-RANGI ZAINEY, indigenous Māori storyteller and healer, mokopuna of the Waitaha.

'The prose itself is a triumph, a stunning reinterpretation of Celtic mythology. The lyrical tone lends a dreamlike quality...beautifully blending the mythical and the emotional. Griffith bridges antiquity and the present, weaving a vibrant tapestry of hope, resilience, and magic...[with] thematic undercurrents infusing the story with urgency and depth, creating a tale as reflective as it is captivating. *The Plain of Pillars* will leave you with a sense of wonder and a renewed appreciation for the delicate, eternal balance between creation and destruction.'

– LITERARY TITAN

'Griffith weaves an epic, dreamlike mythopoesis—a powerful, deeply inspired, animist folktale for our imperiled times.'

– MAREN MORGAN, Death in The Garden.

'Written in stunningly beautiful, descriptive prose, *The Plain of Pillars* uses ancient myth to illuminate modern day issues.'

– JANET ROBERTS, author of *What Lies We Keep*.

'As the old system crumbles, the new will be built out of the stories we tell ourselves and each other about ourselves, each other and our place on this animate earth as conscious nodes in the web of life. If we're going to build new systems, we need old myths told in new ways and Griffith's outstanding book, *The Plain of Pillars*, offers us a grand, beautiful, enchanting story, winding back and forth through plains of ideas and being: new-being and old-being, being as a part of becoming, being something greater than we imagine until it's upon us. This is a beautiful book in all ways, and an essential step in our exploration of who we could be if we really cared about transformation.'

– MANDA SCOTT, author of Any Human Power and host of the
Accidental Gods podcast

. . . past reviews . . .

'Griffith's words are a great call, a nudge, a whisper, and a tap on the shoulder for all of us to remember the essence of regeneration: a beautiful story.' – PRECIOUS PHIRI, Co-Founder of Igugu Trust.

'Griffith has written prose that equals the wild itself.' – ANDREAS WEBER, author of *The Biology of Wonder.*

'Everyone needs to read [Griffith's words] if for no other reason than to honor prophets and poets.' – JOEL SALATIN, author of *Folks This Ain't Normal.*
'An outpouring, a sharing. [Griffith's words] need to be lived and breathed and not merely read.' – ROSAMUND YOUNG, author of *The Secret Life of Cows.*

'If you relish poetic writing, if you delight in beauty, mystery, and wonder, you will dance with Daniel.' – DR. FRED PROVENZA, author of *Nourishment.*

'[Griffith's writing] exudes atmosphere and a deeply felt sense of place, if there were a poet laureate of holistic management, his name would be Daniel Griffith.' – ALLAN SAVORY, author of *Holistic Manangement*.

'Griffith puts into words what so many in the Regenerative Movement are missing. I strongly recommend to anyone who wants to be a part of the community of Creation.' – GABE BROWN, author of *Dirt to Soil*.

'This book is about the core of regeneration. . . .I recommend this book for anyone looking to tend to the wild within and around us as well as engage with the earth in a meaningful and regenerative way.' – DONIGA MARKEGARD, author of *Dawn Again*.

'A buoyant riff that gets to the heart of regenerative farming. Embrace the spirit of this exuberant book and let it take you someplace wild within you.' – JUDITH D. SCHWARTZ, author of *Cows Save The Planet*.

'An impassioned celebration of life in all its complex wonderment.' – JAMES CANTON, author of *The Oak Papers* and *Grounded*.

'An eco-poet and philosopher, Griffith's ecstatic imaginings and lyrical prose don't just live on the page, they pulse in the body. Reading Dark Cloud Country is like watching a murmuration of starlings. The mind swerves. Dives. Rises. It travels to surprising places. The heart too.' – MARY REYNOLDS THOMPSON, author of *Reclaiming the Wild Soul* and *A Wild Soul Woman*.

'Griffith masterfully weaves together history, philosophy, ecology, and literature into one poetic narrative that speaks directly to those of us who deeply love the land. A rare book that simultaneously inspires, educates, and awakens the reader.' – ED ROBERSON, conservationist & creator of Mountain & Prairie.

ffrith, or D. Firth Griffith with The Wildland's Stallion, Amergin Glúingel

Ffrith is a *markâko* and remembering *seanchaí*, a participant citizen of Earth Mother, and a father, horse-friend, sacred butcher and leather tanner, and award-winning indie author of many books on kincentric ecology, mythology, fantasy, horror, and language. Ffrith's books have received numerous honors, including *Independent Publisher's* Fantasy Book of the Year, the *Nautilus* Best Small Press Books of the Year, and Winner of the *National Indie Excellence Award* in Nature Writing. When he is not writing or dreaming with the long–ago peoples, he is tanning leathers, leading sacred harvest ceremonies, hand-hewing log cabins, and running unshod with his three wildlings and wonderful wife.

DANIELFIRTHGRIFFITH.COM

sin magos di klitâns

THE PLAIN OF PILLARS

biwo sin kentus asselî di
sin bandâ-kerdetis natus

BEING THE FIRST RIB-BONE OF
THE RIMWALKER SERIES

UNSHOD**PRESS**

Also *by* D. Firth Griffith

NON-FICTION

Boone: An Unfinished Portrait (2020)
a study of the 'American Man' mythos in the early American west.

Wild Like Flowers: The Restoration of Relationship (2021)
an eco-mythology of short stories about ecological kinship.

Dark Cloud Country: The 4 Relationships of Regeneration (2023)
a philosphical examination of the 'four relationships' of regeneration.

Stagtine: Kincentric Rewilding, Science, & A Tale of Letting Go (2024)
a Nautilus Book of the Year and epic tale of kincentric rewilding.

THE RIMWALKER SERIES: FICTION

The Plain of Pillars (2024)

Bloodless We Go Buried (2025)

The Way of Salmon Moon (2026)

A CELTIC STORY RETOLD

UNSHOD, A DIVISION OF ROBINIA PRESS
VIRGINIA

For information, visit danielfirthgriffith.com.

SECOND EDITION

Published By Robinia Press, Wingina. A division of Robinia Group, Inc., 530 James River Road Wingina, Virginia 24599.

LIBRARY OF CONGRESS CATALOGING-IN-PUBLICATION DATA
The Plain of Pillars: A Celtic Story Retold / by Daniel Firth Griffith. 2nd ed. p. cm.

ISBN-13: 979-8998626517.

For Catherine and Patrick, Margaret and James,
who fought for life.

For Elowyn, Weymouth, and Sequoia,
whose life I fight for. I am grateful that you chose me
to be your dad. I honor your choice, am thankful for
the opportunity to live up to it. Peace, harmony, and
tranquility are just not granted. Listen for your names.
She is calling.

. . .

COVER ART: 'Harmony is Mother's Beauty' was birthed in
the creative dark-waters of co-dreaming between the author
and the soul-dancing, spirit-weaving, color-rattling, earth-
pigment wanderess, and painter, Scarlett Butters.

*Scarlett, my dear friend and found sister, may we always
come home to our shadow-hearth, walking naked the death-
rattle to Tara.*

Nothing in this book is true.

It is not the Celtic mythology your pretty little monks gave to you—a mythology that our pretty little modern mythologists, strangely, see as gospel.

Nothing in this book is true.

A Horse gives birth to a boy, a girl shapeshifts into a Raven, a red hag, and a white Horse, and rocks, trees, and Harps speak like you and me.

Like I said, nothing in this book is true.

But, if you were to think about it, which I don't figure you should, you will see that it is. There is much here that won't make sense. Besides, it is narrated by a blood-beaked scald-crow. Only fools try to make streams straight. Only fools try to understand what is not meant to be understood.

Just roll with it.

Cath Mag Tuired, Old Irish, 9th c. AD.
trans. "Battle on the Plain of Pillars.'

A LETTER TO THE READER

Dear reader, a year has passed since I first sat down to write this story, was once only a dream, is now a highly-awarded second edition that is marred like the green-surf of Atlantic waves on the rubble-shores and reedy-dunes of Dégom, of Earth Mother, by my found sister, the color-rattling, earth-pigment wanderess, and painter, Scarlett Butters. Dark are the waters of rooted work. For its seed has grown. She has found her strata, is bursting now with leaves broad and well-spread. Not much has changed and everything has changed. You are that proof. This is myth. And myth is medicine bundle. I invite you to hold it tightly. And I invite you to hold it loosely. It is a story that describes a world created by music, the Oak branch giving herself. It is a story that tells of a people who listened after years of living in silence. I wrote it as a ballast of breath, a kincentric keel soaking the salt-water, letting in the deep-dark so that we may all float. And so that we may do so together, somewhere more beautiful—and Sacred—than here. A lost brother from another life sat with me recently and gave me many gifts. We dreamed together. Did ceremony. Made many words. And I wrote this letter for him in thankfulness. In reciprocity. And as I sit here writing to you, I realize that I am also writing this for you. My spirit and I are walking unshod up Tara and naked to Uisneach, shaking our death-rattle and wild-carrot both in ceremony. I am unfolding. I am happy. I am coming home. And I invite you to come with me. I am a bastard of bards, a becoming Seanchaí, and this is my gift, my happiness—to bring you with me. All I ask in return is that you never leave. Or leave if you will, but leave your spirit-crumbs behind. The good medicine, the blood-waters for my vampire lungs.

A bite, just a suckle of your waters is all this body needs. Teeth doing that thing like the whale, singing without sound, just song-waves in red waters. If you hold this book, then you hold the good medicine. The medicine of Old Mothers, of the long-ago peoples. The medicine we were forced to forget, but couldn't, not actually, nearly two thousand years ago. The medicine of the long-sleep bear that sleeps with the stag under the snow-cover and snoring-stones. It is a living mythology that I dared not to get in the way of. A preposition ending the sentence, like a breath half breathed, like a breath that I need you to help me with.

Your friend, your kin.

PRELUDE

The last time I saw them, they were blue.

Old canes and powdery orbs held the morning and dotted the landscape that lay under their lurching canopy. Their tears tottered like raindrops in the blue of the sky—or the blue of their falling crowns. Particles finding motion unnaturally but falling anyways. Trees rippling as they splashed against Earth but never letting her go. Not finally.

You can try. You did try. You were tonsured and shaving anything subglabrous. Anything untidy and yet untamed. You tried, and you failed, for they never let Earth go.

The trees were blue but blackening fast.

It was a color one could almost taste. A sweetness punctuating unless ripe. A seasonal harmony discordant without attention. No, it was worse. It was the attention of unkind eyes that chatters in the short days of winter's grey frothy rays that transform the beauty of the winter's deep, resting blue into something else, into something new.

Unkind. The plague rolls.

Unkind. The deaths toll.

Unkind. The blue finding black.

Unkind. The color of the heavens filtering through the Rim of this world, tepid and tidy, when attention becomes profitable.

———————

A gentle mist rose from the exposed rocks like little sentries. Memories of rivers and tumbling torrents echoing upward, first as rounded river stones and then as rising rains. My grandmother told me stories of this valley, now a Mountain, and a great river long before her.

The Land is metamorphosis.

She is kind and welcoming in me.

Stable and unstable if you think about it.

But I think you shouldn't. Think.

Witness, more importantly.

First, the colors.

Then, the roar.

That is what I see.

She smelled the color blue when the river made this Land.

A mountain of cool air waved between her fingers, strange tendrils eating downward. Rising first in spades when she closed them into a friendly full-fingered wave, saying *hello*. Then, ultimately, rusting herself into the new mountains of old leaves slumped at her feet.

Mountains becoming valleys again, soon.

Will the river ever return?

This is where I walk. Most often. I am alone. Always. And I like it that way.

There is something about hopping the scotch of stones and soused ferns under a moonless night's sprinkling and twined light. I am best at night. Some even say that I am the night. There is something silent, full, and free. Something fragrant or flagrant to see. I am happy with either. But you are not.

Stepping the mist, I sing the Sun awake. A pang of bronze often salts the last of his dawning moments before a blue finally croons.

My song is just enough to escort the grey and gleaming away. It is not particularly beautiful, I am told. My song. But it does its job.

I say I sing, but I don't.
I am not that rhythmical.
I am far from sweet.
Not discordant, though.
Croon is just as nondescript, I think.
But my song is not for you.

The last time I saw them, they were blue becoming black.

The stones, so many stones exploding upward. That is really what I saw: a Land braised like beef but with too little water. It was burnt. She was burning. But she also was wet, her years welling at the start, carried in tears, when the engine's purr turned into roars, then steam. So much steam. Falling, always falling.

It does not rise like the mist, this settler. No. It always pillages and plunders the powder-blue and soon blackening canes into pulp. I have heard you say that over half of what you take goes to pulp and plywood. I thought you came for shelter? We would have given you that much.

I thought you came to build a home. Not a tome wrecking timelessness...

The steam does not rise like mist to kiss your cheek. It burns as it falls: when the hot fluids of the machined meet her once living and cool sap.

Magicians in machines,
Magicians holding potions.
Life caramelized.
Not by heat—
Hydraulic fluid.

They knew what was happening. They told me. They did. This was not their first time. Meeting steel. Meeting this noise. Meeting you.

This is why their hearts are hard. But you don't know this yet. And so let me tell you: the trees are growing tired of you, and hardening their hearts is the best they can do. Don't listen to your scientists. It has nothing to do with growth, benumbed sap dying inward, or structural support.

Support? From what? The wind? They call in the wind with song, and they rise and then swell her drafts into great multitudes that glimmer in the gloom. They don't need support. They *are* support.

You are in their stories, which they tell in the autumn, as their leaves drop and as you start to consider them again. Pulled in by their momentary beauty.

Their stories are carried in deep roaring hearts that conserve what little water remains. They learned this the last time you came, and they have held this memory for many mists. That is why I walk with them under the moonless night. That is why I am telling you this now.

When it is not moonless, I fly above them. Looking up at me, they dream past the cloud-spat blue to the black flap of my wings.

They dream of floating, uprooting their earthen and clay-shod roots heavenward, tendrils rotating to reach for the second world, a kinder world, where they will, let us hope, give you a second chance. Maybe not.

Blue, a fine color. Blue, a color of peace. Blue, reserved for those who mourn and worship this ochre life. Those who warm the cold— their epidermal intimacy, their soft touch, their colorful step above ungulate and beast. The birdsongs. Oh, the sapling's cries for the mother tree. The songs. Beauty itself.

Now, today, the silence of machines.

Black consuming the blue.

Roaring a deafness one can feel.

Once, I heard the happiness of children in this wood. It was red. They were content and curious forms that hopscotch from trunk to fallen limb and from lowbush to huckleberry in a loving search for the wonderful and blackless blue of the happy forest. They step the stones like me, but better.

Today, the children were not far away, their sounds said. But your engines roared closer.

A century ago.

A century from now.

Little feet tapping the duff.

And little smiles like leaves, but rusting fast.

A century ago.

A century from now.

Laughter in the lungs, forever an exhale.

Feet tapping the duff, no more.

Today, grenades.

Today, explosions.

Then, red joining the blue and all becoming black.

Within minutes, the blue and red faded as Earth splashed into blackened mounds. Logs of life that were centuries old were piled in neat stacks. Trimmed to neat dimensions. Crooks and knots and burls wiped away like snot. Millennia measured in mills. Ancient life spurting from the depths. Fossils screaming their forest home—their once friends, their old friends that were today their enemies.

Home! The second world. A kinder world. But here, strangely impersonal colors oozed from the rust of ruts, holding water in rainbows, a many-colored and broken promise.

Here, grenades.

Where were the children? They exploded as well, just not yet. Just because they were not here to watch does not mean that your work does not hurt them. You are good at othering and at distancing your work from those it hurts. You are good at many things. Grenades are one of them.

I flew over my friends, the trees, as you drove them away, casting whatever shade I could. I dreamed the color blue, but I cast a delicate black over their slack and now stacked bodies that sang the colorless day into its final death.

You tell me that I am death, and one day, I will tell you something as well. Just not yet. I am more gracious than you think.

As I flew with them, I wondered about the pain you humans must live with. I wondered when they would stop forgiving you—you mammals hiding behind machines. You mammals hiding behind your stories and religions and settler myths.

They rode on, these trees, my friends. They did not even try to roll. I would have rolled. I would have tried. They did not.

Why are they so giving? Forgiving.

They did not try to tumble into a roadside trench. Curling fingers of roadside corpses with flies that divide and spray when you saunter by. No. They could've, you know? But they don't. They didn't. They stayed stacked, their truth chafed and imbrued, mile by mile, their memory forgotten but not lost in mills.

When will they tell you?

What they really feel...

When will you ask?

———————

This story is not my story.

It is yours and it is told for you.

I tell it. That is true.

It is not mine, but it is my gift to you.

My only hope is that you hear it and, in hearing it, you see it—this ancient and peeling leather book that sits gently on your nightstand.

Acknowledge.

That is: see.

Then attend.

Before it is too late.

The trees are kind.

But the god's forgiveness wanes.

There is something else I must tell you before I allow this story to begin: you are in great danger.

This story is an exercise of the open heart-mind.

The finer elements are easy to miss, like the beat of your heart, if you are not paying attention.

The dream that crafted this story holds the story. To read this story without dreaming is to hold a rock and never notice the world within it, to hold in your palms the Waters of wells and never notice the tadpole yet to be born that wiggles here and there.

Much is left open in this story, and what you need is given to you in dialogue, for that is how I know what I know. I only rarely see into the heart. But I hear what is spoken, and I have excellent hearing.

You will see this story as either true or pretentious: that is also the danger.

If it is true, it is true because you are willing to look at a tree and say, "Hello." More so, you are willing to acknowledge that your simple word, the world carried in those two humdrum syllables, meant something to the tree as much as it meant something to you.

If it is pretentious, it is pretentious because trees do not talk, and stories of talking trees are hurtful because they are wrong.

If you find this story true, welcome.

If you find this story pretentious, welcome.

It is for the all of us.

PROLOGUE

He was too close to the man next to him to smell the blood rivering down his forearm. A weathered old hand of war, he grimaced only slightly as a tapestry of arrows reverberated overhead, piercing the air and whistling to finish what others had started.

"They talk, we fight," the veteran next to him whispered to himself. His shirt was torn at the seam, threads broken and bitten through.

"But we are here. We may as well win," another man laughed to himself, a breathless bubble rising in his crooked neck.

"We will die," Luchta muttered back, his eyes scything across the line of hunched soldiers. There was drawn anger, empty scabbards hanging loosely below empty hearts.

The men around Luchta were painted in crimson with striped and symbolized sketches etched across their already blood-crusted and spear-shaved faces. Symbols that mattered when war was a contest in fearlessness. Symbols that mattered when battles were fought between men and not for men.

But today, it was to be a mêlée to scythe souls. A devil's mirk, rent beyond repair.

Behind them sat men on horses with swords, and behind them sat great men on great horses with no swords at all.

Men leading men from behind. Stations and ranks defined not by accoutrements or valor or skill, but by the lack of red, like ochre paint, that spilled around them.

Another volley of arrows ricocheted in the cloud-spat space between me and Luchta's men.

That's right, I am here too.
I am the Raven above the field of battle.

The landscape was a patchwork of infant woods and limestone shelving wolds, still undecided if they would be glens, meadows, or moist moors.

"Moist moors," I thought as I flew above it all.
Tonight, they will be moist.

It was evening, and the grey light was abating fast. Soon, a red Sun would rise above the open plain to the west, and the battle would begin.

"You are the son of a god?" the man who stood next to him inquired. "Do you have no power?"

Luchta did not answer.

"No," another returned, angrily and answering for him, "he is the son of a wri—"

"—a wright that was a god," the first asserted quickly and without turning his attention to the second man. He was tall and carried a long scar down his exposed chest, browning as it aged, a remnant of a rusting spear that came close to edging him away.

Luchta was quiet. His heart was elsewhere. A fungi finding root, it sought the rolling range of the bald Mountain that overlooked the great wolds of his peaceful Land. An upturned island, the Land under the Rim of the world waved in multitudes of grasses and river reeds that sang with the willows' many wands in a revering rhythm. Music was everywhere, and the soft winds carried her song. This was the Land of his life, and it was this Land that his heart sought.

He held memories clad in mist and deepening dusk, covered, just barely, by the upland forest's moistening duff. His family would often venture to the edge of the rock-scared cliffs that overlook the great plain of their people or the great wolds that echoed their chimney's breathless gauze back to them in order to witness the grandmother's rise. Their people held the Moon in common and often found her night-water intoxicating when steeped high in the heights.

They would walk to the cliff's edge and then turn around, placing the plain far below to their back. The Mountain's supple and cool breeze would waft them eastward and up into the settled nests of the Crow-Ravens.

Their hearts becoming full in the Moon's night-water. Their hearts becoming high on the Mountain's loving heights.

We would dine together.

On the Mountain, they would visit me. At home in the village below, they would close their eyes and fly with me.

But today, their eyes would be rent from their bodies, and I would descend to walk with them, stepping their deaths together.

When Luchta looked back over the events woven through his life, these were the deepest. Like the oak on the Mountain, his memories drew down past the stones and their stalwart agelessness into the heart of the Land. An unhewn dolmen, the seat of grace, the living marrow of their life's music. The village. The clan. His family. Her face.

Lips a supple pink, tasting the fire's winter red heat. Her heart, a deep pounding red, reflecting shimmers of yellow and bronze against the once pale hearth. The eggshell color of her words. Her life planed and now curling in his arms. Her lips, fibrous and playful. Her calloused hands feeling his.

Her arms now waving him home.

His visions disappearing into a grey mist.

———————

"You are Luchta, then?" the man next to him inquired. The man paused as if to think, to taste the thought for its salt. He shifted his spear to his other hand, gripping its shaft a little higher. His forearm bulged red under the strain. "You are Luchta, the son of a god?"

"It is true if you say it is," Luchta replied without looking. His eyes were busy and shut. He was dreaming of the valley's wind lifting with laughter, and he was dreaming of flying with me. "You are right," he replied as he opened his eyes after a moment, reality snapping like bone.

The wind's clap on the cliffs distilled with a white snap, and the waving music fell into the parched Land at his feet. The sounds of children echoed outward and away. Always slipping away. The rolling range of the Mountain and the Moon's night-water and his family's fired hearth, memories that had colored his vision, fell before him and disappeared as the sullen and swollen plain solidified. Then, dullness and focus. Fingers wrapping not around wood or shaft but wrath. Metal clanging on shields. Hearts closed under chain and mail. Anger rising like rain but sour and red.

"But you should thank my brothers, the smiths of Art and steel, for today, they are all you have," Luchta muttered.

No one heard him.

Mountains of soldiers shuffled, and a great dust drifted over the stifled plain. The men in the front suffocated. The men in the back were pierced by arrows. A worm inching forward but losing its tail, the copse pushed forward in a violent panic and men fell over each other, toes kicking heels and men kicking men.

Those with swords and on horseback circled to the left and gathered into a charge.

Then, dust.

Screaming Earth.

The great moor opened for its quenching.

The moistening began.

And then, red.

It fed me for days.

————

The battle began in a rush of hoarse laughter.

Guttural shrills screamed legs into the dust, a hurricane throwing debris back on the Land. The sky was quickly clearing and the clouds reclined. The dusking Sun, now red, shone brightly in the west, but the Moon was quiet and dark. She was not interested in culpability, so her face looked elsewhere.

A deep clamor panged across the plain as the two armies met each other at first in theory and then in reality. The enemy's forces seemed to have swelled in the reddening dusk, and Luchta thought he could see even more men filtering in through the valley cut behind them. An infinite mass of men ready for mayhem to etch its face upon this strange arena.

Men clad in heavy panoply swarmed about the Mountain's feet from end to end. Their lines stretched the width of the plain, and it pulsed like a wave on a pier—in and out, swirling at times.

Luchta's line stood, waiting. A volley of arrows released from behind them with a shrill that cast many into ruin, but their enemy's ranks refilled quickly like ocean sand and then appeared to double. One down, two in their place.

A clamor of color rose to meet me, and I flew higher to avoid the arrows. I am not impervious to your pain.

I landed on an exposed and phallic perch just above an escarpment of river stones. A perfect pew to watch. To bear witness.

Oh, how I watched hungrily.

The enemy charged first. Their great host roared the sea. Their ranks collapsed nearly into a single file like a host of ants following the scent of death.

Deep drums echoed commands, and they waved over the plain like the tide. Slowly at first, feet stepping the rhythmic *boom, boom, boom* of the deep—a song that only sailors feared. Until today.

They surged in mounting steps with banners pressed forward. Their long spears held at the waist beamed a white light under the red westward Sun. The butts of their spears sat in leather cups sewn into their belts, freeing one of their hands for fighting and the rest of their body for spiking and thrusting. A full-bodied press, their onset would be fierce. Some carried javelins, and others carried blunted instruments, striking death with mighty blows. Destruction living in the descent. Others even carried horror itself.

They charged, curling like gravity. A force ready to crumble like feta off its block, and some were crumbling even now. A deep *doom* quickened their pace, and the mass cantered, closing the space between.

A hare loosed to the left, startled. It was huddled in a patch of heather that was attempting a settlement, purpling the bog with teardrops fashioned like bells. It rang with every step of the advance, signaling for life to leave.

I saw it run.

I saw its fears. I wanted to give it wings.

I heard its cry when it was smashed like dry sticks underfoot.

"There they are, the many of them," Luchta's superior asserted as he rode in front of their line on his brown war Horse.

She brayed under him. Although young and fresh, the Horse was clad in greying metal and leather billets fraying after years of stropping. The campaign had cost her rider seven Horses, all shot out from under him, and the men started to wonder if he was a god.

"If he was," one man whispered, "he would protect his Horses."

"If he was," Luchta muttered back, "why would he need us?"

The drums stomped faster with a *doom* and *boom*, and the ensuing hurricane gathered into a twisting stampede of rain, wind, and debris that stumbled forward chaotically.

"Today, this evil will die. Let us give it to them, men!" the horseman screamed as his Horse reared onto its hind legs, bouncing up and down like a top. "Whatever happens, men, stand and fight!" His words trailed downward like stones sliding into a pit as he galloped off. No one seemed to believe him. The line seemed to take a step back.

The dust was almost eye level now, and her floating particles suspended specks of light in twisting and twinkling collections of red and orange. Squinting, one could almost see flecks of yellow dotted with ochre reds and silty seafloor browns. If the poets were here, these would have been colors to write about. Alas, they were shot through last week for their bardic powers were greater than their fighting skills. The poets' necks and chests had lengthened to find the air above the miasma, and her arrows landed to give it to them. They laid with papers strewn across their chests, black ink spilling red around them, a fifth appendage shafting breath anew.

Luchta's eyes fell to his right and saw continental mercenaries on horseback gathering to flank. They twisted and circled in anticipation, stamping their hooves clean of the day's muck. The strange men worked to stay aboard the jerking and twisting mares, each whickering the adrenaline outward. The riders carried long swords crafted in the ancient technique with thick, straight blades. Weapons to cast blows and strike steel. Weapons to provide contest. Weapons of Skill and Art.

But today, they would slice like hasty butchers.

The brown Horse and her rider were gone, drifting somewhere into the rear, out of range of arrow and lance.

"They talk," one man whispered.

"We die," another returned.

———

It was not long until their line broke.

Luchta leapt forward, his free arm splitting the forest of thrusting spears aside. He heaved his weapon deep into the skull of another. Its edge split the helmet and his force ushered from handle through hilt fractured the neurons. Sparks flew like heated iron against Earth's anvil when man met man.

I could see it from up here.
I could.
I felt bursts of heat when sparks sent souls my way.

The message was clear and cast salty liquids like falling Waters that pooled at their feet and dowsed the smiting smiths. Luchta slipped to a knee, the soft white becoming a solid brown when the stale muck converged with the buckskin covering his legs.

He lost his spear in the mud. He must have dropped it when he fell or when the sparks burst deafening colors. Crawling feverishly, fingering for the metal and wood, his anxiety admixed with terror when the pulsing mass above him began to move laterally.

A *doom* echoed above and through him. Another *boom*. Then silence.

"Another charge?" he screamed out loud. "Why?" he demanded in words reeking of pain.

He scurried below as the muck of the filling red pond grew deeper. Chaos chortled through him and overtook his senses. Another soldier had fallen nearby, a young body brimming with arrows. It was the man that had been next to him in the beginning, the man who thought of gods. His body now slumped forward as though praying, seated on a stone ledge and overlooking the mangled corpse of a young girl.

Luchta's last sight was the man's blood flowing into a fall from the arrow's fletching into a hole in the girl's skull. Every patter, a splash. Every splash, a network of ripples over the landscape. Red, her brain mixed with the mayhem, the muck.

And then the muck rose to meet him. A great, flat foot was thrust into his back, and he fell face-first into Earth. At once, the rippling stopped. At once, the mayhem stilled into perfect silence. The greenish and toeless hoof sent gangrene up his spine, and then everything was calm.

His heart knew movement—he could feel the retreat. His senses felt vibration—he could smell the drum's second charge. The devil's mirk, writhing and wiggling. He could not move.

The charge ricocheted the line backward, the men recoiling against the surging wave. The Company wedged their spears behind them for ballasting, but the curling shape of the consuming wave consumed them. Feet slipping and men falling, twisting and becoming flat under the metal soles of already petrified souls.

"Stay strong, men," the superior's command boomed over the field. It was a strong voice and carried on trumpets that blasted positions and movements that no one could hear. What was to be never was had.

"Stand firm!" It screamed.

"Sweep left to close the punctured whole bleeding the enemy through."

"Pivot to brace the flank!"

"Form ranks! Shield wall!"

Voice without avail. Voice for souls that were already gone. They were overtaken, and their ranks collapsed like the rings of trees, readable only in death and readable only when it matters not at all.

A pond of miasma, a crusting entrail slithering itself straight. Thousands of men and women crawled like crippled insects, and some even were missing torsos. They walked around while others fought beside them, looking for their stomachs, reeling them back in like eels.

They tumbled over their heads.

I hopped the scotch of men and enjoyed the putrid potpourri that exploded like grenades when my claw punctured with a pop their swollen bellies. I tasted green and smelled the already pulsing white wiggles of life locomoting in the legless and writhing millions of maggots.

Larva making life.

A metamorphosis twisting the fibers.

Will they remember?

Will they ever?

Men converged like a nest of twigs, overlapping often with limbs so entwined that biting was all they were able to do. Noses and ears dotted the landscape like stumps, and many were discovered in the days that followed with their heads plowed in the dirt. Inverted bodies swelling in the heat. The last effort to get away, it seems, a frenzied and freakish attempt to become clay, sooner.

One man writhing, still, his face in the mud and sinking under the retreat.

A muffled malaise drowning on once dry Land.

Then, stillness.

The battle raged in colors even you could have tasted, but he was still, his legs flapping only subtly as the mortis set in, his outstretched arms with hands clutching the last bits of Earth. The black muck filtered through bloodless fingers, his body oozing downward, becoming clay, the worms swelling and swimming upward.

Luchta, the wright, the son of a god, was dead.

He drowned in the dirt.

Aboy was born that day and a thousand years more from the yellowing mane of a Horse.

He arrived with dirt in his mouth.

I, the blood-beaked scald-crow, or Raven, must stop this tale already to prepare you for this story, for it is otherwise and unlike many that you tell yourselves.

This story is of a time when moments made the seasons. It is a tale that plays strangely with time, for there are no ticking clocks, no Moons made by months or months estranged by even stranger gods. For this people, for this story, the silvery-white Moon was good enough, the Sun's daily birth sufficient, and our own gods, nameless though they were, were solvent.

This story is about a Land out of time—a vision within a dream. It will not make sense unless you enter this world fully or remake your world into it. I am fine with either. That is your decision.

It did not take long to bring him into this world, not at least from my perspective.

The mare stomped up the Sun and rolled violently in a carpet of mugwort, releasing a caged dream in scents like sage. The writhing created a soup of smells that floated about her like a veiled mist and blanketed her work with secrecy. She savored the sweet dream, which was vivid and real, and she rolled and writhed when she met it.

To the east, the tumescent arm of the Mountain stretched to a stop and shielded her from the descried landscape beyond. One peak rose above the rest. It was large in complement to the surrounding dales and minor summits, and its outflung arm created a labyrinth of shade and focused light. The bald Mountain was bare save for the strange figure punctuating its apex. The figure spread its many arms as an overturned bowl and looked lovingly upon the wide landscape below. It was regal and alone.

Black godwits nimbly negotiated the borders of the moors and edges of the lesser pools that lay below the Mountain, and great numbers of oak and willows littered the moist spaces where the Land rotted apace, and the nut-brown bonneted mushrooms rose invariably.

"The Dear Mother," the mare said to the mugwort, laying on her back and fingering the papery patch of pinnate green floating around her. Both a carpet and a blanket.

"As foals, we dreamt of floating up to visit with her when the mist was heavy in the morning and after the midnight storm had made the Land a slipshod terrain," the mare remembered.

A slight breeze shuffled and scuttled over the mugwort's leaves as the mare spoke. They twisted from green to white and back to green again.

"Mist that floats even the rooted upwards," the mare whispered.

They lay together, the mugwort and the mare. The wind feathering up the valley and across the plain. They looked east and up.

"That was a long time ago. My great, great grandmother took us there, once," the mugwort said. Shivering, the memory slithered up her spine and her leaves tingled under the old energy.

The mare smiled in return.

Together, they fell into a long silence, an ancient dream descending into stillness, a simple hypnosis where images become real and the real become dreams.

The mare laid her head down in the grass to share in the ceremony. "Do you think she looks down here and thinks the same?" she questioned.

"To walk down here? I often think she gets lonely. All with roots think about these things," the mugwort responded.

"Lonely," the mare said. Neither a question nor a statement. Just a word, an artist, clad in white robes with brush in hand.

"Yes," the mugwort said. The breeze again twisting her leaves lovingly. White and green paling into each other. Two becoming one.

"She couldn't be alone then." A smile crusted over the mare's face, and her two great nostrils flared with laughter. A smirk enjoined the conversation to close, and they laid together the afternoon long.

"On summer's eve," the mugwort said just above a whisper, when the day's darkness began to settle, "we sit and watch the Sun's set reflect against the alone tree, the *Máithrín*, the Dear Mother, and on summer's morn' we watch him burn her alive."

"An enflamed sacrifice to the gods," the mare responded.

"No, to her friends," the mugwort smirked and then was silent.

———

The outflung plain under the Mountain was reticent.

Streams and valley moors shaped like spearheads thrust into the rocks and rocky earth that just a few years ago rolled under a great river. Its Waters were dark, a deep blue and clear like evening light witnessed from a yet lightless room. Life filtering through glass, an unflurried face, and still. The Land amidst the Waters was now a grassy sward upon a mottled plain that shelved down from the Rim of the world.

I want to tell you what lay beyond this Rim, but you wouldn't believe me.
I have so much to tell you.
Alas, you are not ready to believe, for you are not ready to see.
But we have many lifetimes.
I am in no haste.

The mare's black mane yellowed at the tips when the Sun rose, and she stood up, her medicine complete. The dream descended back into Earth, and the mugwort flowered into little ivory spears. A two-way instillation of fertility. A single orgasm. Life reborn but not remade. Life together.

The mare was the sorcerer of the Horse clan and often enchanted even the Sun to dance. She was known to gallop into a cresting wave in the early morning hours of the moonless night, and the Sun would rise to join her. When it did, time slowed down. When the mare rested, time ran instead.

Fields once replete with stillness exploded yellow and purple flowers when she walked by. Even the stones sang their granite and lime songs when she waved past.

This morning, by the time I landed near her, the boy had been born and was shimmering. I found her licking him dry.

"His name is Long-Arm," I told her, looking into his heart.

"Yes, *Lámfada,*" she returned without looking up.

The mare was smiling.

Life was thrust through the ether for another chance.

Why Mother gives you so many, I have long questioned, but that is not my role here: to question.

I am the boundary walker, the mischievous one. A trickster trodding the old road. Often rogue, I carry her alchemy.

But I shouldn't question it. Life, I understand why she gives that to you.

But her grace is impregnable.

Not long after he was named, the mare brought the boy to the long house in the center of the village.

The great wooden doors yawned as the mare stood on the threshold. The air of gods silently filtered beyond her crimson silhouette.

She carried the babe on her back and lowered him to the floor, bending her great knees to feed him. He suckled wantingly. The diaphonic song of nourishment filled the great hall.

An old fire roared its ashes in the blackened stone hearth at the other end of the gallery, and a funeral of smoke lingered, both dying and already dead. She whickered without looking, and the ash became charcoal and then salmon-colored oak once again, sending flame up the chimney. The fire quickly worked against autumn's coolness to warm the space. With the smoke now rising up and out, she again lowered herself to nurse the little one.

The mare unwrapped the green and woven covering—given to him by the mugwort—to reveal a paste-white cage of bones, itself wrapped in soft human leather.

"One day, we will run together," she said as her nose tickled his belly.

"One day, I will beat you," the boy replied back, reaching his two small hands into her great nose-tipped muzzle. He tickled her into a sneeze.

They laughed together.

————

In time, how much is unclear, her mane returned to its black. It happened slowly and simply. The sable smells lifting once again and floating away like black eagle feathers when she waved over the Land.

The People of Síraide, the village of our story, lived as the limbs of the Land's many colors. When the child was born and delivered to them by the Horse, The People gathered around the wooden doors of the great hall and offered the Waters in a clay Caldron. The Waters were from the sacred river Cailleach that flowed beyond the village and supplied them, and the many strings of ancestors that came before them, with water for drinking and water for guidance.

They dipped the boy's feet in the clear liquid, and a peculiar energy rose through him. Herbs and their aromas flowed into his lungs and then out his ears like the fire's smoke in the living-stone chimney. Mushrooms were brought in for the baptism.

Pryderi, his mother, the mare with a magikal mane, backed away and watched, smiling.

The People placed the boy in a phallic bed of interwoven fungi and covered him in the living bark, the cambium, your people would call it, of the Oak tree. The Mothers worked endlessly weaving a mantle of brocaded silk and sinew to wrap around him for his first sleep. They worked fiber over fiber, interwoven and sticky, inviting the spirit into matter.

"She did wonderfully," the oldest Mother said as she carefully handled a strand of sinew, separating it for the woman next to her.

"This was a big decision," another Mother responded. "This little one must be special."

"I wonder what she saw in him?" the youngest Mother, Bacharigu, the most recent inculcate, herself born of the Bird, questioned. Her eyes drifted through the pearled glass window and floated into the meadow beyond the hall. There, she saw Pryderi, who was silently grazing the late summer grasses exploding one by one through the once-green carpet of yellow and bronze.

"Bacharigu," the oldest Mother asserted quickly but kindly, her eyes never lifting from her work, "that is not for us to question."

"Yes, Old Mother," the girl returned, her eyes still out in the meadow.

"What they do is up to them and their relationship with One. Do you understand?"

"Yes, Old Mother," the girl returned.

———

That is how the child was born, and that is how he was welcomed into the village.

Now, I must give you the story of his inculcation.

That morning, while The People dipped and covered the boy, Teyrnon, the Ardent and Stag of the village, laid an altar in the plain beyond the long house. He then worked day and night for one year, hewing the Mountain for her stone. A ceremony of drumming, of inquiring stone from stone, of erecting a pillar on the plain, his great antlers crashing into the Mountain's face, repeatedly. With every collision, the loosed mineral's smell drifted over the valley in a blue-grey wind, and a subtle rhythmic *boom* lulled the child into a deep sleep.

The boy slept for two years.

During the first year of the boy's sleep, in the early winter, after the veil was torn and their year passed into darkness, The People of Síraide lit fires around their Ardent and danced. It was their reasonability to keep him warm. They consumed the snow in colors of yellow and blue and imbued the portal and soon its pillar with the color of life—green, a living dolmen.

In the summer, The People carried the Waters from the valley and spilled them around Teyrnon's hooves, creating a slurry for his work, like the amniotic that passes when all is complete.

Teyrnon crashed continually against her face and questioned her, praying for her stone—the heart of the Mountain. Soon, when the end of the first year dusked upon his work, he sculpted her largest gift, a blue quartz, into a shallow bowl to place atop the pillar to complete the ceremony: the sacrifice.

The People then dispersed, and their traditions disseminated like broadcast seeds as they filtered through the forest to gather her moss. For another full year, they worked to unfurl moss from root and stone, and some even, typically the youngest, dropped curling hairs from the top of the moss-aged boughs of their oldest elders. The People crawled and ran and slithered and swam under the great cathedral. Soon, after a year's time, they gathered at Teyrnon's raised pillar and covered it in their moss.

The shaggy green mat then grew legs and sunk its tendrils deep into the stone. Pryderi stood with the boy on her back and shivered an energy that worked inward. At this, the boy awakened.

He incanted,

And I behest the beast,
Charging, I bend sinew from stone,
Growing, I belch spent breath anew.
From old moors I betide the world,
The secret pools that heath on stone shape soft.
I am.
I am the thunderous surf, the sunlit dewdrop.
I am the placid lake, the rushing river,
The Caldron of Cailleach,
Swimming from the Otherworld well.
The deep and rusty blue valed voices,
I am the god who gives you fire.
Who knows what is beyond the great Rim?
Who announces the ages of the Moon?

At this, Teyrnon stepped forward. A Stag naked against the year and humbled without his armaments. He placed the crafted stone bowl atop the green pillar. The People of Síraide marveled at the perfection of its shape and its redolence of their plain—for it contained two valley cuts that would allow a clear liquid entrance into the bowl and then a red magma to exit on the other side. A little rimmed world inside their own, a harmony sculpted in gifted stone, the heart of the Mountain at once above and within their own—the plain and its pillars resembled each other in a perfection only an ardent artist could achieve. Not even a smith throwing in heat or hurricanes could have crafted something so perfect, so beautiful.

The oldest Mother then strode forward, slowly, carrying the now stagnant yet herbal Waters of the Caldron, a brew two years in the making.

The People watched as the Old Mother entered the center of the circle and stood with the pillar. Her form now redolent and becoming seamless with the stone.

Teyrnon bowed his head, the many scars echoing his ageless work, and Pryderi whickered a flame into the bowl. The Old Mother poured the liquid slowly in the northmost cut of the stone, and a deep drumming distilled upon The People from the lone Mountain above them.

A *boom* fell like a stone avalanche, and the vale veiled behind a deep mist as the liquid began to stir and steam in the bowl. The fire worked upon the Waters. The pillar resonated a bottomless harmony with her Mountain mother and released a drumming that shook the mosses and the lichens.

The fire heated into the color blue as a new and red liquid pooled out and down the lower cut of the stone and onto the soil at their feet. The People danced and shook and stomped when the red solidified into a coagulated corpus.

At this, the Mountain fell silent and ambled back into herself. The wind and lapping flame stopped. The People stood still.

Long-Arm, the boy, walked forward, leaving Pryderi and dropping his brocaded covering, his silky skin and sinewy legs now fully alive.

"From vestige to verve," he recounted from a deep and unknown memory, "we, the dancers, the desert forestall."

"To *Fódla* and her sisters," he continued after a moment, holding up an earth-fired clay cup of red and circling to show the village above his head.

"To *Fódla*," a chorus returned.

He lowered the cup to his mouth and smelled her contents with an impecunious inhale. He choked on the aroma which percolated through his body like a song—from the Robin's ancient music, where The Emergence happened all those mists ago—life from nothing, a creation through the plucked strings of the Harp, of gentle, resonant, mellow, sharp, crystal, splashing cascading strings.

That is how the world began, and this is how his life rebegan.

But I am getting ahead of myself.
  That is not a tale yet told.
  Let me get back to the story.

The boy took a heavy draught and fell back. It was clear and cold, the once red liquid, and he drank and was satisfied. Once again, the stone's liquid thickened back into red when it fell inside his empty cage of bones, landing in his stomach and expanding like a balloon.

It curdled through his colon. It drifted outward like gas through offal walls and flowed through parched veins and empty chambers and ventricles, four of them to be exact, and then it began: the pounding, the thudding thump.

He was alive. Or, rather, life was now his to share.

The People then dispersed and went about their common lives. The ceremony was complete, the visions were experienced, a new year was born, and new life was at hand.

He laid there for yet another year, curling under the great pillar's roots that wound down to the river Cailleach—the great river beyond the village. He lay and was still, allowing the burgeoning silence to mature.

This is how The People welcomed life.

––––––––

The best things cannot be told. The second best are only to be misunderstood.

  Years from now, you will wonder about these strangely wonderful people. That is why I am telling you this story. Their strangely wonderful story may mean something to your strangely abysmal and modern life.

  They are wonderfully strange, and I got to witness this wonder first-hand. You could say that I illustrated it, but you could not say that I orchestrated it. That would give me more credit than this trickster artist should lug about.

You'll listen to books blaring above your machines, and you'll read two stories. One was written by a social colonizer, the other was religious. You will praise the prophets and priests, but you'll never meet us, the shamans. We lay under your many feet. We are colored and not consumed, but we are struggling in your absence.

Will you?

Become less absent?

Archeology will try her best but will aid you little—what does a clay-covered sword say? It was living once, the sword, and it had a name. But you do not know this because you never asked. And we do not tell you because you were never kind.

Will you?

Be more kind?

We are a shapeshifting people living on our feet, those who fell from the stars, alive with a ceremony of days.

We are animate animals. You wouldn't understand unless you do, but then again, if you do, then you already did.

Our bodies are surrendered stars. Light at their end but also, soon, a beginning. Exploding, we die over and over, and that is the role of the pillars—to live once again.

We are a people between worlds, this world and the Otherworld, where space and time are liminal at best and hold no consequence to the story of our lives. But our pillars are still here, erect little mountains calling back their cores. Mosses eating their way with roots sinking into the stone.

Whatever we left has long reincarnated, metamorphosized into something, someone else, as soon as we dropped it. That is the point of dropping things—to let them go and to let them become something new so that you can soon follow.

Even the pillars you mistake today as mounds. The mosses growing on them exemplifying their age. What age? They are there because we asked them to be, invited them with blood and bone and ceremonies now long lost.

What does age have to do with it?

What is the point of this life, you ask? I have never thought about that, my Crow-Raven and trickster brain is too small for your big questions.

But, if I were to answer for you, I would say: to drop it and to see what it becomes.

—————

I have told you about the way The People welcomed life—the Horse, the Ardent, the pillar, the plain, the Water, the dancing.

Now, let me tell you the way their life was destroyed.

Around this time, the Land looked upon a sea in perfect calm, a waveless board in an ocean of trees.

The elemental powers of fire and earth, the spirits that haunt the forest and streams, knew not this shadowless form. It was strange, the great calm that echoes without words and purles over still waters.

"Wind waves over land and water, but a water without breath is a land without life," the Land muttered to herself.

At this, the Sun glittered a yellow and soon whitening light upon the glass, and a violent wind fell from the cloudless sky. Rocks tore their tendrils loose, and trees unfastened their leaves. The wind tore at the Land. Life purled into a violent tempest. But the Waters remained still. Unnatural.

The winds abated instantly as if turned off by a switch, and there appeared three sisters. Sovereignty goddesses—the Land with legs.

"Something is missing. The void is a vacuum pulling us in," the oldest sister said.

Energy splashed without ripples, and the sisters felt drawn, sucked nearly, into the Waters. Their chests bulged forward like a fist punching from the inside.

They stepped forward. They nearly fell forward.

The youngest sister, with red-gold hair and a tan tunic that extended into a long train behind her, flung her right hand over the sparkling stillness. Words inaudible to ears and without a syllabary for eyes muttered in waves under her breath in the old language.

At this, the sea floor shifted slightly, curling over itself, and a shallow reef formed. A white thread, a long thick dragonfly brocaded past on silver gauze wings, and the sisters' eyes followed it out into the Waters, but no surf rippled beyond the reef.

"Grandmother Moon has no power here," the youngest said. "She is weaving, but no garment is shaped."

The middle sister returned, "The guttural respire upon Mountain stone that ricochets our song upon the wings of the dragonfly, Grandmother Moon's fluttering fingers, is empty. She is not illustrated here. The music, the Harpist, is asleep."

The oldest sister then replied, "Some strange evil walks here. It works the Waters flat and curses even the sea to anchor."

In truth, these sisters are gods.

In their love, long ago, even before I came to this Land, they decided to clothe themselves in clay—to walk with us and to be walked on by us.

For all the occult arts at their helm, it was their delight to be of one heart with the Land and her Waters, her winds and trees that step the mammals into being.

It was their delight to be both god and man.

The three sisters stood on the edge of the ocean and beheld the foreign energy like a magnet on metal.

"A sign," the youngest sister whispered to herself as she stepped toward the Waters, her feet floating on the sand. "Like blood drawn from a wound but peculiar and calm."

She looked into the ocean.

Somewhere across its silent waves a weight, a shadow, a glimmering in the doom, the deep rising to the surface. She beheld a vessel of silvery light drifting upon the moonless Waters. It was neither pushed nor pulled but strode forward on a strange stream. Its size at first was great but diminished as it neared into the shape of a man.

She stepped forward, alone, into the calm Waters, pulled by a nameless rip current. She submerged her ankles under the shallow bay.

The man was now floating close to her. He was of the fairest form and golden-yellow hair shined upon his head and fell beyond his shoulders. Gilded trimmings adorned his shirt, and equally golden threads dotted the brocaded silk with reflected sunlight. On his breast was a brooch of gold that encircled a center stone, a sapphire, that shined of the deepest ocean water. In his hands were two white-silver spears.

"I saw your spears from afar," the youngest sister said. Her eyes stayed on the silver, and a fine blush welled into her cheeks. The water felt strange on her ankles. "I thought they were a vessel carrying a soul upon my shores," she admitted.

"No," the man said, stepping forward. "They are a basin for the basis of my travels."

The Oceaner then dropped the spears into the calm sea water that existed between them, and a great wave echoed in opposite directions. It curled a strength hitherto unknown. It pushed the Waters outward, an underhanded and unexpected current ripping and pulling the Land with it.

They were both drowning in the deep water.

"Is this the time that our lying together will be easy?" he asked.

"I have made no promise to you, Oceaner," the Land returned, gurgling water from her lungs and struggling to stay afloat. She was drowning, fast.

The waves rolled her up and down and cast her about like late leaves in the winter wind. She tumbled and spun and drifted for time unknown until the waves calmed, and she found herself once more upon the sand.

Her white shirt, now skin-tight, splashed upon her back as the waves traced over her with searching fingers. Her own hands curled the sand. She lay face down. Down as though studying her face in a dropped and now damaged old mirror. Down as though dying.

Her eyes fell down and saw a golden thumb-ring that had been placed upon her middle finger, and no matter her efforts, she could not take it off. No matter her attempts, the water's bloody memory sunk like tendrils into her.

"Verily," she contended, now crying hysterically and standing up, casting her words over the now waving sea beyond, "this tryst of trickery is against those who have entreated me in vain: my sisters, my people."

The Land wept the ocean anew. The Land wept and the sea rose and crashed. The Land wept that she was possessed so quickly. The Land wept, and she stood up with crossed legs.

"Breoch," the Oceaner's cold voice returned from beyond the waves, "the beautiful, the shapely, he who was made from the sand-kissed and wave-born tryst of trickery. This will be his name," he said. "He was made to destroy your world."

"He already did," she thought to herself, the words red in her throat, shame falling into her gut.

She did not feel beautiful.

Four years later.

The Mothers were like shamans or priests, but they were not shamans or priests.

Like, I said.

Bacharigu, the youngest Mother, had never lived in a place that was this temperate—she had never lived in a place for long. She was from the great mounds beyond the Rim of their world.

Mounds that you call fairy mounds, but she was not a fairy. She was a Mother, like I said.

She arrived around the same time as Long-Arm, the boy born of the Horse. She was the same age as the boy, but their paths rarely crossed. She walked with The Mothers and was herself a Mother, although she was quite young and unpracticed in their Art.

It is generally assumed by anthropologists and their pupils that the ancient villages of this world were small and isolated communities where everyone knew everything, and everything was shared by everyone. This may have been the case for some, but it is surely not the case for all.

———————

The Rimmed world of the Síraide was a Land of old moors and networked hills that careened and rose into the rocky face of the bald Mountain. Eternal river valleys and misty mires snaking silently below.

Wherever one walked, it was moist and cool, always playing with winter. Ancient trees, older than the crop of man, rippled over the Land in small patches. Their roots so deep that it was said by the Old Mother, now half-lame and one-eyed, that when it rains and the thunder flickers and flaps, bouncing flares down their cambial sap, that their roots are sprinkling down to wash us.

A circular cleansing, the roots, at first, sinking into Earth and then rising as they fall from the heavens. The rain, their roots, reaching for us, completing the circle through the heart of our world, the soil.

"We are in and of the circle," the Old Mother said as she and Bacharigu strode down the center of the town's greenway. Leather tents, or *lavvu*, peppered the road on either side. They were constructed of rough animal hide and dried grasses, their frames requiring only sticks for support. This gave the *lavvu* a particular portability that The People depended upon.

When the rains turned into torrents and the great Mountain screamed new rivers down into their valley, The People would pack up their accouterments and move to higher ground. When the rains settled, they would return to the valley.

Like the seasons, their lives tottered in the liminal space between here and there, between being fully present and presently flying away.

"The Trees shoo us away, we like to say. Sometimes, they need a break from us, and the Mountain beckons a respite," the Old Mother said to the girl Bacharigu. Her dialect was lilting but stumbling and rhotic, which fell away from The People's straight intonations. Her speech was peculiar and very old.

She was smiling with her good eye closed, squeezing a slight tear. A memory of torrents and falling rains washing into her emotions.

"A respite?" Bacharigu questioned.

"The Star Oak," the Old Mother said as she pointed across a bridged arc of stones. Mathgen, the sorcerer, rolled the stones from the Mountain many years ago to make simple the crossing of the Glei, the small stream flowing through the valley. The stream always found its strange way and wound through the center of the village, no matter where The People placed their tents that season. It followed them like the Star Oak. It was living and changed how it lived, like The People.

"The Star Oak is the reflection of the *Máithrín*, the Dear Mother atop the Mountain, and sends new stars every autumn, building new worlds with a flutter of her limb," the Old Mother said.

The Star Oak was ancient and sat in the south of the village with her gnarled and outflung arms cresting downward like an overturned bowl. Infinite nests and hives accumulated in her branches, and flakes of grasses and wildflowers hung from her greenwood.

The Horse would hang Gloriosa daisies with their lone black and dangling eye surrounded by a bed of yellowing pedals. The Stag would tie the red and black witches' poppy found in the rocky uplands to the west. The Robin would place the meadow's silvering milk with orange crowns, and the Crow-Raven, I would place something else.

"That feels right," Bacharigu said. "She sprinkles with a shake and we dance and harvest her bread."

At this, the girl's heart wandered into the fire season, and her fingers throbbed and began to hurt. A memory of biting sap when the acorn's shell sliced under her nail, the color of sand and dust staining for weeks. She smiled, the memory laughing her gut awake.

"Yes, that is true—but it is even more true that when we leave, removing our tents from this valley, our bread becomes her little ones." The Old Mother spoke with her fingers dancing in the air like playing children.

After a moment, her fingers still playing, she continued, "Sometimes she gives. Sometimes, she does not. And sometimes she gives, but not to us. Do you understand?"

"I do," Bacharigu nodded above a thick smile, her eyes lost in the Old Mother's capering fingers.

———

"The circle," their people would say musically to each other during their migrations.

"Roots reaching for us," someone would return.

"The Mountain is moving closer, and we are thankful," another would say.

"Look, see! She lifts us downward," someone would beckon with raised arms.

"The circle," the chorus would continue.

When their tents, or *lavvu*, began to rot, typically around The Two Fires Ceremony in the spring, The People would burn them and start over, a craft that took the summer.

The *lavvu* was less vertical than that typical outside of this world and could withstand the great winds that tore through the valley in the autumn. The Síraide learned this building technique from the migratory hunters in the north isles of the world far beyond the Rim.

Those who run with the reindeer and those who taught The People their Art long ago.

Bacharigu walked with the Old Mother through the village.

The tents were moving in a strange motion and caught the girl off guard. They were alive, pulsing and pulling the early morning awake. The green aisle avenues that wound through the heart of this season's encampment were littered with families carrying sticks and rolled leather bundles. Children were encumbered by mats of tied grasses, and the youngest walked with hands full of their favorite rocks and gnarled tree branches.

Everyone moved without lag or labor, but there was a somberness that was otherwise unfelt during Bacharigu's time in the village. Faces defeated by some external violence and faces that carried a brisk tinny timbre reticent of the rickety lilt of lamps that dawdled in the rafters of the long house. Lamps that were illuminating and extant, but odd and unnatural as the wick worked downward by sucking the oil up.

The young girl felt this solemnity as an ungrounding gravity, like a storm. It was as though The People were used to it but not used to this. As though they were well-practiced in the Art of migration but unwilling to practice the Art this morning. A seasonal harmony discordant under unkind eyes, a sweetness punctuating unless ripe.

Some tents, those higher on the hill, were still covered in sleeping dreams while others, those lower in the valley, were busy ripping their roots free. Something was causing the lowest clans to migrate higher into the heights. Something was drawing them. Or someone was pushing them.

She was confused but did no more than offer silent questions, for she carried the Caldron and her fingertips shook into a pale white under its strange and shallow rim.

"To remind us of our own world," the Old Mother instructed, pointing to the rim. "The deep cavern represents the stomach of Earth, and that ledge there—"

"This?" the girl questioned back, pointing with her eyes.

"Yes, about halfway up its belly. The great Mountain's heart."

"I see," Bacharigu returned.

"The Caldron is open not in want for the filling but for acknowledgment," the Old Mother said without looking. "For us to acknowledge, to attend to her, to visit her to the Waters of the river Cailleach, from whence we all came."

"I understand, Old Mother," Bacharigu said.

She did not.

Not truly.

Not yet.

They walked beyond the many clans and their devolving tents to the great river that undulated westward and trickled in pools that were deep and cool. The Glei flowed neither to nor away from the great river Cailleach. They were not distinct or divergent bodies of Water but carried their Waters in diverse ways—the Glei ushered Earth's underwaters into the moors to live in puddles and bogs while the Cailleach escorted the Mountain's Waters from her heart to the ocean beyond.

When it rained, the Cailleach cried in torrents of flooding Waters and would often sift over rock and bending blade into the Glei, animating her gentleness, giving life to the lesser stream, the moors then reincarnating into lakes and ponds. For the moment.

"It welcomes the underwaters into this world," the Old Mother said when they walked beyond the lesser stream that trickled through the village. She was pointing to where the two bodies pushed aside their Earth in cutting banks to meander their snaking bodies toward each other, like magnets and metal.

She continued, "The sinuous curve in the channel that bends there: that is where their energies are the closest."

The young girl twisted her head gently in question. Her hands were still busy carrying the Caldron.

"The Mountain's heart, kissed by the rain, pulls the Glei upward and then, in a flood, smashes her down," the Old Mother said with a feathery wave of her hands.

"What is wrong, Old Mother?" Bacharigu asked, nearly bursting with a glum curiosity after holding the question for long enough on the tip of her tongue.

"What do you mean, my girl?" the Old Mother questioned back, inserting a homely serenity in her words. A peace that was unsettling.

"We collect the river's Waters when someone is born."

"Yes—"

"And we collect the Waters when something is wrong."

"Yes—and you wonder which it is?" the Old Mother asked simply.

"Yes—the clans are packing their tents and migrating higher. What is wrong?"

"We know the seasons change when the great river lifts the lesser. We acknowledge this shift by attending to our tents, moving them up the Mountain."

"Yes," the girl responded, "I understand. But it is not raining and the seasons are not shifting."

"That is true and it is not true," the Old Mother continued, now shifting her weight. "The Mountain's water is not littering the meadow, but something—someone—is forcing our leave." She paused and gathered a breath. A pungent sulfurous perfume of unnatural air tasted upon her tongue. She whispered without exhaling, "The plain is becoming a pond."

The girl was silent. She tasted salt in the air.

———————

Distant from the village and now encased under a canopy of trees, they approached the River at the meander.

Yellow light filtered through the loose canopy of oaks that dotted the riverbank. In the shallows, ancient white willows with their deep and furrowed bark grew in patches of two or three with the fig-mulberry, which cast green balls of burr-like fruit into the water like a child casts wishes.

At the river's bank, Bacharigu stooped over the dark Waters. She breathed deeply and watched the current spin leaves and white washes of foam. The Old Mother's words floated in her mind.

The plain is becoming a pond.

The Land was parched after the long summer that fell headlong into a dusty and dry autumn. The soil crumbled between her fingers when she sifted it gently, and even the meadow's grasses that danced above the moors that lay behind her were browning early.

Becoming a pond.

"But how?" she thought out loud. The season seemed discordant with itself, nature out of sync and outside of her own pace.

To her right, the river's pools were dark with the bated complaints of frogs. A bird, unknown, plunged the thin willow branches down and exploded in whistles of whipping leaves as it passed. Life astride the river's Waters was both quiet and explosive, and the quiet explosion clothed the girl in irony. She felt happy but also felt distant from having happiness like rain must feel in clouds. She felt home, and she felt strangely far from home.

She had set the Caldron down behind her, now a few paces upstream, on a flat moss-covered ledge of flood-cut limestone. Looking down into the river, she at first saw nothing but black folding below the cut riverbank. Exposed roots extending outward. Waters flowing inward and curling into the darkness. Then, slowly, she saw a form develop, and the deep Waters encircled her sight in waves like a frame.

A sycamore ball had dropped from the tree above her head and splashed into the river, raising the Waters in plumes of small white flames and cresting foams. It plunked into the depths like a sunken jewel.

At this, an image developed and waved in front of her. The Mountain appeared within the rippling Water, and then, after the image stilled, she saw the lone tree extending from its peak. The great tree, the *Máithrín*, seemed to be waving at her. Limbs bobbing in the current. Love framed in foam. Beckoning to her. Calling her by name in a voice inaudible and indistinct like the pale-pink morning mist. Then, the Waters became a bright blue. A sublime blue, the color was matched immediately and equally with bright stars glinting a fine white in the image's blue sky, and the great belt that retained their heavens was visible, strangely and unnaturally, and reminded her of a wagon's tracks after the rain.

Though she looked upon the waters, her shadow or reflection could not be seen. Some Art was at work.

"For pains and aches of body or heart," the Old Mother said, placing her hand on the willow tree's trunk behind her.

The girl's vision evaporated instantly as she turned and watched the Old Mother sink her fingers deep into the bark's furrows like a lover well met in intimacy drifts their verve over the curves of another.

"Now, it is your turn," the old Mother invited, her eyes staring deeply into the girl. Like the tree in her vision, the Old Mother's eyes pierced her chest in languages felt but never heard, understood but never known.

Bacharigu shifted her attention from the river and picked up the Caldron. She looked on and engaged her eyes into the grey and moss-covered tree. She looked. Her eyes scythed and slashed below the bark. They looked to see what was not there to know, and she looked with her heart first. After a moment, she closed her eyes and concentrated. Deeply. Holding the image—the green tendrils fluffing a living duvet across the grey skin, the sunlight sparkling shadows that dappled the shifting grey bark into infinite shades of aromatic waves. She breathed, pulling the air in and letting the ether that was pregnant with fungal spores trickle and saturate her lungs. Then, she let it all go.

She stood emptily with her eyes closed and her hands by her waist. They were open. Palms outward. She was ready.

"Focus," the Old Mother's words echoed from trunk to limb, the last syllable snaking from her tongue. "Attend and dismember yourself." Again, her words snaking and slithering, finding Bacharigu.

"All I see is black," the girl blushed.

The Old Mother, her fingers now embedded into the bark, was solid and still but bright, like stone in the summer.

"Focus—release your fear," she said with pursed lips.

The girl did. One thought at a time, she let it go. Acknowledging, like water over cascading stone, she touched and let tumble each thought, every aspect of her little life, in a cruising current of washing memory.

She became perfectly silent, and the black she first saw became a liquid that surrounded her. She dropped the muscles in her face one by one and felt the sublet of tension that subtly constrained her body release as her attention fell downward. It landed in her feet, and once collected, she pushed it through and out her muddy toes.

"Thank you," she found her heart saying to the color flowing from her feet. "Thank you for being here, your many staining and sacred particles, and thank you for leaving."

She did not know why she was speaking, but she spoke, and the words felt right. Weightlessness exploded like torches blazed with light—like light beaming into dark places. The ground rose steeply behind her eyes, and she floated in the falling limbs above her.

"Fearless," she whispered after an unknown time. Then, she opened her eyes.

The Old Mother was gone and she was now standing alone, firmly, on the riverbank.

Her gaze scythed across the river.

It searched through the trees.

Her teacher had vanished.

She was alone but not lonely.

And so her eyes closed again.

First, black. Silence and breath. Then, a heart-sense rose and pounded in her chest like incense beckoning to burst. The river at her feet, their roots now entwined, the willow, the river, and hers now sinking deeply into the unknown depths. They swirled into a tornado of watery leaves. A spark, then many, surged through Bacharigu's body from her toes inward. From her gut, it worked upward until the fluid found her neurons and pulsed the color green—green like leaves but clearer, more honest, and intimate. Green like the rivers of cambium that flow below the bark of the oak and willow weave that ushers the river Cailleach upward.

"Below the bark," Bacharigu muttered with a sharp snap of consciousness.

She struggled to open her eyes but achieved the feat after a moment of rubbing and twisting her knuckles over their lids.

The river was calm. The trees windless.

"Yes, that is where she gives us the medicine. Good," the Old Mother said, a spirit becoming visible once again.

She stepped from behind the oak. Her ancient and bare feet ambled gently over the autumn litter of nuts and fallen branches. Her silvery-white hair plaited now in a mingled and mixed way. It flirted with regality. A flower tucked in a curl, a leaf twisting from a loose knot, a furrow of moss that was reaching its life deeper into the beautiful and silvery-white duff.

The trees and their river were alive and sinking their roots into her.

She looked different, even Bacharigu thought so—prepared for burial, almost, and beautiful. The Old Mother was as a corpse readying for its realization, a body whose expiry beautified its end. A death song worthy of a chorus.

The Sun seemed to rise and set but without the regularity of routine. It was as though a handful of moments, to be what they needed to be, required many days to pass in order to manifest the magik.

"Her magik—" the girl began to speak, questioning now what she saw stepping around her. She was drawn to the Old Mother in a new and strange way.

"No, her Art," the Old Mother interjected immediately. "Magik is nascency, the dawning of Creation without light. Art is the correspondence of Creation, the harmony of the Music."

"I see. Her Art," the girl continued, blushing a new redolence, "was clear."

"What did she tell you?" the Old Mother asked as she looked up at the kissing canopy.

"To prepare," Bacharigu said without knowing but also knowing all the well.

"Prepare?" the Old Mother asked.

"I need to find Pryderi's son," the girl returned, looking beyond the river and her forest, deeper into the valley where the bald Mountain found resonance in the standing sliver of Long-Arm's silvery stone.

The yellow light grew broader and less fine the deeper the river became, and even the Ancient One (who it is said burned their ships under a dense mist when they first sailed up the Cailleach and into this valley epochs ago) had never met the depths of the river's bottom.

"Why is her name Cailleach?" Bacharigu questioned, kneeling beside the deep pool of broad light. It was only a few moments after her willow wand vision, and her legs remained unstable.

The Old Mother was beside her, doing the same. They were looking at themselves, together but also individually, in the clear clean water. The uneven surface of the tumbling torrent confusing, at times, into a mirage: two forms floating into one body, two heads becoming one, two journeys colliding under some unknown and future flood.

Bacharigu's body was shivering.

Blushing.

Hairs standing straight.

Back arching backward in the vision's pleasure.

But warm. Kind.

She was sure.

The Old Mother never answered her question.

She was busy filling the Caldron.

The girl knew why.

"Will I—" she asked.

"In time." The Old Mother traced a circle on the girl's back absentmindedly. "Soon you will be the one. You will step forward when I fall back. That is why I've called you here."

"To the river?" the girl inquired.

"No, to this world." The Old Mother smiled.

"Why?" Bacharigu almost asked. A confusion needing straightened, something important hinging on that question, though she was still unaware of what it might be. But she was silent and willing to wait.

A moment hung white in the morning like a web that was strung but now stranded between them. The Old Mother gazed wistfully upon the river. Bacharigu looked pensively at the Old Mother. They both smiled.

The Old Mother dipped the Caldron in the Waters, and they walked back through the willow and oaken copse, the river at their backs. The green moss now loosed from the brown bark and flittered like fairies in the dancing light. The Sun was still rising in the east, finding its routine once again.

They strode back through the tents with new eyes. The young and Old Mother hurried on with urgency.

"Every family, extended or otherwise, lives in their own thicket of animal hide," the Old Mother said. "Each abode decorated with the insignia and color of their matriarch. It goes like this: *Horse*, the yellow-black Pryderi. *Stag*, the red-brown Teyrnon. *Robin*, the oyster-orange Harpist. *Plant*, the pale-green Leech. *Crow-Raven*, the black Mothers."

"I understand," the girl returned. She nodded her head blankly as though a student being instructed on the basics of tent-building.

"Listen," the Old Mother said in a whisper that caused the young Mother to step closer beside her, to lean in eagerly, "this is my last lesson: the plain is becoming a pond, but it is not the pond that you must consider."

"I understand—or, really," the girl said, "I mean, what must I then consider?"

"You," the Old Mother returned without effect or emphasis. Her eyes were fixed on the rising Sun.

"Old Mother?" Bacharigu's voice punctuated the stillness.

"Yes, my dear."

"What lays beyond—" she paused, fiddling with the world in her mouth and the Caldron's rim in her hand, "the great moors and the Mountain?"

"The Sun," the Old Mother returned simply, laughing the morning awake.

The boy who fell from the yellowing mane of the Horse grew two years for his every one on the mare's milk. At seven, he held the mind and strength of a fourteen-year-old, and his skin leathered under her tutelage.

The boy and the mare ran together, unshod, over the fields, and the wind carried and echoed their laughter up and against the Mountain above the plain. They would run and laugh and their laughter would lift the soused meadow grasses up again. A community dancing together, a community of kindness healing itself.

They visited his pillar often, making sacrifices of Earth and Water. Pryderi would place flame in the bowl, and I would visit with them there.

"Do you think she feels us, the *Máithrín?*" he asked, his heart drifting in the ceremony and his long arms extending like two spears tipped with feathering fingers to the tree rooted atop the Mountain. "The valley trembles when we run. Do you think she feels it?"

"What do you think?" the mare questioned back. "The *Máithrín* sees much."

"She visited me in my dream last night," he said, blushing an intimacy otherwise uncommon for him. His cheeks becoming red, his eyes casting the blue of the flame back on the bowl.

"And?"

"She said hello," he paused. "That's all."

"Then she feels you," the mare smirked as she kicked up dust and ran off, getting a head start.

He ran after her, blushing another smile.

————

His limbs grew longer than the other boys, his metatarsal bones extending out of his feet and into his legs like a horse. He was not unnaturally long, just longer than the other boys and so they were happy to call him Long-Arm. It seemed right. And boys, lost in their boyhood, often like what is weird but seems right.

His half-brother, Miach, born of mugwort and not the mare and a couple of years older, was a medicine man and cared for him often.

"And? Where did you get this one?" Miach seemed to ask on repeat.

"We ran up the escarpment to catch the Sun's set, Pryderi and I, and I tripped on a loose stone. Lime, I think." Long-Arm smiled at his brother, remembering the warmth of the setting Sun on the stones under his naked feet.

The grey becoming gold in the evening light.

The smile becoming medicine between the brothers.

Long-Arm placed his hand on his brother's shoulder, the touch vibrating a peculiar energy between them—the roots of the one grounding the galloping grace of the other.

"What do you think is out there?" he questioned. "Beyond the Rim? She never takes me there."

"More, I would imagine," Miach said absentmindedly. He was busy attempting to stitch Long-Arm's leather back together. He was able to stifle the blood that his brother had lost, but the full repair was taking more energy than he had to give at the moment.

"More of what?"

"This," Miach said waving his free hand about him in a circular fashion. He talked often with his hands, and his hands talked often for his mouth, like leaves speaking in the wind. He continued, "Mother mugwort reminds me of my roots, sinking deep into Earth. 'They are not tethers but tendrils for exploration,' she says, and I think about that, you know?"

"Yes, I know," Long-Arm replied, a dream galloping inside of him, pounding his heart with its pulsing.

He did not. He knew only little of roots sinking and searching into the dirt.

"To know is not good, to explore with uncurling roots—ah yes, there it is—done! You are healed. I think that stitch will hold—but you have to rest!" Miach said.

"I will," Long-Arm replied.

He would not. And they both knew that this was true.

Miach strode off to his cupboard, around the back of the room and through a narrow channel of the hall, and a peculiar smell wafted back. The aroma of herbs filled the void left by his absence. The medicine man was gone, looking for one last thing, but the medicine remained.

—————

Long-Arm sat at his brother's table waiting. The medicine man was slow in coming and so his mind drifted in the other direction. It fell outdoors.

Looking through the rough window, Long-Arm saw a Crow-Raven perched on the branch of the young oak that Miach's father had planted as an acorn the year before he left. It was about as tall as Miach and growing fast. The bird's black tail was spread in the wind like a hand of cards, and its dim eyes fizzed under a strange curiosity.

Long-Arm, still looking out, felt himself both drawn and otherwise to its power.

Cían, Miach's father, was also a healer, or leech in the old tongue, and Miach cared for the family's apothecary, adding to it and imbruing upon its strangely infinite depths with new medicines, constantly.

Miach was often absent from the village gatherings, lost in the lower hills and river valleys collecting flowers and making ceremony with his cousins.

This is how he made his medicines—

by communing with them.

This is how he healed—

by healing himself.

He was a member of the Plant clan, which was also known as the Ambassadors. Cían, their clan's leader, departed with the other healers, medicine men, and poets, such as Cairbre, to engage the Oceaners in dialogue nearly one year ago.

They were never seen again.

Or, at least, not yet.
But that is getting ahead of myself.

The Oceaners were The People's imperial masters that levied monarchic and foreign rule over them since the days of their colonization—when Balor, their god-king, arose out of the windless Ocean and swept the Land's sisters in waves and pillaging plunder. Following this despoilment, the Oceaners then imposed odd limits to The People's years and levied unnatural taxes upon them. They removed them from their old language, forced them to cut their hair, and denuded the Land's Art into knowledge. This is the process of colonization: language, identity, and then relationship.

But this is not why Cían and the Plant clan ventured past the Rim of their world to speak to them, to plead with them. No—the Oceaners were not generous or honorable, and that was enough to incite cause.

The Síraide's knives often left the gatherings ungreased, and their tongues never smelled of ale. When they met at the yearly meeting and tax collection, no poets or bards, neither the Oceaners singers nor pipers nor their fools or jugglers amused life into the meal, and a deep sorrow sunk into the marrow.

One poet of the Ambassadors, Cairbre was his name, after a sullen black gathering, lit by neither fire nor wax, and after a meal of dry hardened cakes, incanted a shamanic satire upon Balor, the god-king.

He said,

Without metabolism moving on dish,
Without the honeyed milk whereon the calf may grow,
Without a bed of oak kissed by the meadow's marrow,
Without story hearth-swollen in reddening flame,
Let this be your pain.
Let no days see the roots of rain.

Cían's embassy ventured into the Underworld, intending to dialogue over this lack of hospitality. This is the process of freedom: relationship, identity, and then language.

No one ever heard from them again, or their poet.

"Oh, you'll enjoy this!" Miach's words slithered down the hall and drifted excitedly into the room like the morning mist.

But Long-Arm did not hear him. He sat perched with his eyes outside. A wintery gust of wind sent red leaves from some unseen green grave skittering beyond his view. It then fell back on itself, somehow righting its course, and filtered aggressively through the window, clustering his face with the aroma of autumn. The short gale seemed to push out the original smells of the room, and the color yellow settled in their place. Wafted back into his chair, Long-Arm looked through the rough glass to the tree. The bird was gone.

"Was it ever there?" he wondered to himself.

The branch bobbled. Her many small limbs wobbled a new nakedness as they undressed slowly before the coming season.

"This is wonderful," Miach spoke to himself this time as he entered the room holding the medicine. "This year's harvest of garlic chanced during the Moon of mists and rain. The river Cailleach burst her banks, and her deep-blue and rusty river muck flooded the fields.

There is rich, black Earth inside of each clove!"

His excitement boiled as he chopped a handful into a glass of golden sugar. "Garlic, muck, and honey—is there anything else?"

"The color of wind at full speed," Long-Arm whispered to himself, his eyes still peering out of the window.

"What was that?" the medicine man inquired, twisting his head a degree.

"Nothing. Never mind. That looks wonderful. Thank you."

The night before Bacharigu visits the
Cailleach with the Old Mother and the
Caldron.

A silent shadow flitted over the Land and crusted a memory of the sea in mounds of salt behind his webbed feet.

The village was asleep and slumbering deeply. Their sullen murmur seemed to make the pregnant stillness both humid and harsh, and even the Moon was faceless. The once-roar of the Land was now silent in the slumbering darkness, carried only in dreaming breath, like the cold drone of distant cicadas. A yell into a grotto, a shriek of shrill, a moment rumbling against an eternity carved in stone, but miles upstream and unheard.

The silent figure swam from tent to tent, peeling flap from leather and exposing those sleeping inside to the night-water, the somber timbre of the moonless dark.

The true black. A color created in the Underworld. A color dependent on the heavenless night. A color reliant on a silent Land of music-less shadow. A color unnatural in this world or the Otherworld.

Not even a flitter of stars was awake as witness.

Macguarch, a chieftain of the Oceaners, was sent by Balor, their one-eyed god-king, to steal the Harp of The Síraide. His job was simple: find it and take its music.

————

Before we can continue with Macguarch and his dark night deed, we must learn how our world was created.

All cultures, ancient or otherwise, have their stories.

All stories, cultured or otherwise, have their power.

This is our story.

The Harp was carved from the first oak tree that lived atop the unformed world. This was long before she, as you would know her today, was formed. Precious stone jewels were then inlaid in the heart of the greying wood, stones lifted by love from the heart of the Mountain.

It is said that the great tree gave herself to her people. The Harp was the form her love chose, for she loved music, and in love, her music was made.

On the first morning, near the Sun's rise but during the cold moments just before, she lowered her branches and fell. It was subtle. It was nothing particular. Trees during this age gave much to us, and they were happy and honored to help us grow.

Her delicate splash rippled over the formless space, and a mist swelled like a bloated corpse under the battlefield's Sun. It covered the Land like breath and hovered, waiting.

"Every Art reveals the artist," she whispered to herself, and an expression of prophecy came over her face. "Every artist is alive in their Art."

Her ripples, the swelling mist. This was the first song that lifted the Land in littering notes. Then, out of the mist she arose as a beautiful and well-formed Harp with her sinew as strings and her olive cast heartwood as the pillar and body of the instrument. The pith, her heart of hearts, perfectly encased the brace—the outer echelons of the instrument's anatomy.

She was to wear her life in reverse—always out, always present, but never clear. That was Creator's gift. Her many green and gauzy leaves impressed in the soundboard gently and gave form to the many pins and levers, their curling petioles ready for the tuning.

The tree then gave herself fully into her work, for she was lonely, and the Harp was just the beginning. For many empty days, she walked across the Land, dreaming forward her friends. Her sap she gave to the wells for streams and rivers. Her acorns she gave to the Mountain, and their cupules tumbled into upturned valleys. Her whitening bark slid like tumbling rocks and became the lowland moors and marshes, bogs to hold the water and bogs to hold the curlew's song.

The inlaid stones were given to The Síraide by the Mountain herself. It was said that when the great song called the Land upward in rising torrents of creative fire, the great sheets of ice that once sheltered this Land under a great cold coat receded to the north.

In the oldest of days, she carried her *Song of Tonn Tuaithe*, a harmony that surged like ripping ice and falling rippling Waters that held our ecotone's memory of Creation: of forming, of her unlonely love that cast all into being. We sang of the cirrus back-draft and aggressive down-cut of the animate ice that shaped our overturned island, or world's Rim, and we sang her praise for many generations.

When the Harp was complete, there arose a Robin, the Harpist, who sang,

We will make together a harmony,
A great wonder, an interminable flame,
Under the heavens, your love will sing,
A life harkened by the Harp's great strain.

To this, the Harp then replied,

To you we give our music,
Our power the love adorned theme.
Our melody enough,
A woven beauty—
Sinew in sinew,
Bone in bone,
Blood in blood,
Together our world its color will bud.

At this, a sound ignited like that which had never been heard before, and intersecting melodies that bartered and meshed ushered the Land into being. A great transposition, the veil between worlds fell, and the depths became audible as the dwellings above and below were filled with overflowing colors.

A perfect music floated above Earth.

The Harp played a *wail-strain*, and the Land wept in piles of ash and glacial rock. Torrents and gurgling shakes ushered life from the great exposed chasms of the Otherworld and shaped the Land as it danced, frolicked, and quivered in the song's shamanic possession. Rocks tumbled into hills, wells like swelling tears combined into streams, and streams into great rivers. The Waters carried stone and seed and the landscape's chaos ushered the context for life.

The Harp then played a *sleep-strain*, and the Land cooled and fell back into silence. Two-way dream walking, a peculiar and personal harmony oozed like cold lava over the landscape, and memory unfurled in two directions. A subtle mist covered the Land for an untold number of years, and the Harp's strain animated the welter and unformed waste. Life rose and fell rhythmically. It pulsed with the beat and pluck of the string and the headwaters of the Cailleach collected. The mist and collecting music planted an oak tree on the river's bank and then dropped an acorn into her shallow Waters with a ruffle of her green feathers. The first ripple, the first life plunking in the depths. The silent and formless current carried the bronze orb downstream and cracked its shell upon the rocks, kindly breaking life open for the sharing. The river then ascended out of her banks, holding the many pupate oaks, and they, together, covered the landscape with green.

The Harp, at last, then played the *smile-strain*, and life laughed into being. At first, the river-carried oaks created friendships with the soil and soil friends that flow like muddy rivers themselves below the Land's surface, and then willows and ash, colors and sound, followed. The aroma of air under gauze and feathered wings flapped and clothed the Land, and bees shouldered their way through the long untrod grasses to taste the flower's erotic song. The buzzing flitted like stars around the dusty horns of the ungulate that supped with the lion. The Land danced when it rained, and the ancient caverns of falling rocks were filled with the roots of the living.

That is when the Harp and the Harpist looked down from their heights and understood their relationship over all of the substances that danced below them.

Life smiled tears dry when the Sun rose, grew when he enflamed the day long, and slept at peace when he fell. Every day, a creation anew, from the exploding and evanescent wail of the Sun's rise, the riant smile of the day's growth, and the formless and drifting sleep of the misty night.

The Harp and the Harpist.

The Art and the Artist.

The Sun and the Day.
The Moon always.
All grew in kindness, and all grew within the circle.

This is how our world came into being, and this is what Macguarch, a chieftain of the Oceaners, was here to take.

———————

It did not take him long to find her.

After looking within the tents of The People, driven more by a childlike curiosity than a mission intelligence, Macguarch followed the melody of the *sleep-strain* that hovered over the village in a silvery mist. The doors of the long house were open and waiting for him, and he gently pushed them aside with his large webbed hands.

I landed on the great Ash outside of the window of the long house and looked in.

I was only curious.

I had no mission other than to observe.

The doors creaked a minor scale above the tonic, and he ambled forward into the dark. A subtle trail of crusting salt slithered behind him. After finding white, it then fell back into a blue liquid once again. His path paved ponds.

———————

There, in the deepening shadow of the hall, in the corner opposite the hearth, the jewel-sparkling and oak-greying Harp saw him. She looked upon him and saw him for who he was.

"The evil have it simplest in this world, if you ask me," she said.

"I didn't ask—" he replied listlessly against the dark.

"They sit at ease and gape not at themselves," the Harp continued without letting him finish, "for their fate is of little worth to them."

"We gape at you," he returned, closing the chasm of the hall between them.

"Magicians gape at their creations, but they know nothing of Art," she laughed.

A subtle shake quivered the dust awake that lay upon the floor in neat piles. A little wind trickled through the dim space and played with the now sparkling dust like a child with rocks.

"And if you know nothing of Art, then you shall never know defeat. Isn't that something? We need both to have the one," she said after her loving and dusty laugh was complete.

"You are something," Macguarch returned. His eyes were fixed on the particles.

"Yes. Perhaps," she said, "those who never know think they know all, and those who know all also think they never know."

"Never know what?" he asked. His words seemed rung out of him beyond his will, an unexpected curiosity.

"—Me!" the Harp returned with a harsh austerity foreign to their meeting as her music crescendoed to circle the dust, now at his feet, into a tornado.

The rushed melody created a black hole in reverse, the weight of everything at once casting debris in the wrong direction. A great creative noise cascaded into blasting winds that colored the hall in a fine white light. It was not anger but intense love that bore the light and shook the dust.

And that is when I saw his eyes for the first time, looking in from my branch just outside the window.

They were red and reddening fast.

"There is another world I hold in mind," Macguarch said, breaking the silence that followed the storm. "A synchroneity of the bitter sweet and dear grief into a pain of longing for a dying life or a living death. Sorrow lives where death extends not. Pain lives where she is never complete. In this," he said with his webbed hands motioning to the long house and the sleeping village around him, "let me have my world to be damned with it or to be damned without."

His speech seemed rehearsed in some practiced way.
Even I saw that. Stagnant and stale, like the pond of salty ocean water growing at his feet.

"You seek a singularity, some simple arrangement," the Harp responded with gentle clarity, "but to realize our nature, what we hold in common, is to hold the music herself."

At this, she plucked a single note—the high C, the root chakra. It danced the dust into a two-dimensional standing wave, a pattern of visible vibration, a star encasing a perfect circle. The Oceaner fell back, startled and struck somehow by the pattern of her music that was now walking amongst them. Breathing his breath. Music now moving visibly in this world. What should be inanimate became animate and threatened, kindly, his heart's existence.

He stared at her music's marvel, and he could do little else.

"You see this world as an image of paradise," the Harp continued. "But we see this world as paradise."

Holding the high C, its perfect pitch shaking now more than just the dust, she said, "Your existence speaks that another exists. Our existence speaks that we exist. You look to the heavens. We believe that the very nature of existence is heavenly."

"No," he returned, taking a step toward the Harp.

At this, the music fell, and the dust settled into a perfect quiet. A strange windless hush filled the void. Uncomfortable, unnatural quietness.

"To influence is to give your soul. To acknowledge is to keep it by giving it away," the Harp returned, looking at the settled and still dust.

"No, we just take," Macguarch said, ambling another step toward the Harp, reaching out his arms.

But she did not run or turn. She could have. She could have escaped with a flit of her string. Rather, she smiled and leaned into him. "Influenced, one does not think their thoughts. Their sin is not theirs; it is borrowed. Their music becomes an echo. A putrid, mock harmony," the Harp said with a tone of question. "You will never see because you are afraid of being seen. Is that why you came here invisibly?"

Macguarch was silent, breathing a deep pause, his form shadowless in the dark night-water. He was prepared to accomplish the task given to him. He was prepared to steal the music, the Harp. He was not prepared for this, whatever this was.

"I am jealous of everything whose beauty lives and then dies," he said after a while, admitting some ground. He did not know why he allowed the space and the conversation to live as it did.

"Then you are jealous of none but yourself," the Harp returned.

"How do you mean?"

"You never live—"

"I am here now," he said.

"You live everywhere but also nowhere. You have made relevance irrelevant. Love loveless. Life listless," the Harp said.

Defensive and growing now more so, he screamed in welling anger, "We live in a light filtered through the depths, tipping the liminal one way or the other."

"Yes, a language that speaks only in universals," she said calmly.

"An evil that pulses through raised follicles, your listless and unliminal life."

That is the joke, you know?
While they pause in the dark long house and as I look in through my garden window swaying on Ash, let me tell you that this is the great jest of culture: it tells you that life lives by tipping the liminal one way or the other. That life lives by being alive.
Ha! I will spoil it for you: it does not.
Life is the liminal.

The Harp again plucked a single string and then muted the sound and its reverberation. The wind rose and then stopped instantly, and everything fell back to where it was before. The dust sparkled dimly as it sprinkled back into place.

The fireless hearth burst spontaneously with a singular flame filled with an effeminacy hitherto only held by The Mothers. The burst of silence ricocheted against the angular building, a noise that lifted a wren from her nest that was wrapped in the ceiling's exposed and twisting cruck blade.

A hollow color settled in the silent darkness.

Black greying into red when white was cast upon it.

———————

They stood in silence for a period of time, Macguarch and the Harp. A pregnant silence, a pupating period held in a cocoon of silent silk.

After some time, the Harp chuckled into laughter, and then she saturated the hallowed hall of the long house with a *smile-strain.*

"You do not acknowledge the life around you, and so you will never find yourself," she said. "Your pain will never complete." She was smiling. Laughing and lauding the moment for what it was: the end. Then, she fell into a *sleep-strain*, and the room's life dropped into the dust, nearly napping.

Macguarch was silent. His anger still but not distilling.

"You are afraid that the Good is good enough," she said after looking directly into his red and reddening eyes. Her words made them crimson.

"Good enough for what?" he responded quickly, awake and now fully upon her. His hands cresting around her neck, squeezing the tuning pins loose. Her music dropped and became flaccid.

The room seemed to shift, to fall, into a spineless slack, a dawdling limpness without life.

"In this way," she said without vigor and ignoring his question with a jarring bluntness even I could feel through the window, "you will never know yourself. You will never be whole."

"I don't intend to be whole," he said with his one free arm twirling around him, indicating his body's mutilation. "The waves deface even the strongest," he said.

Macguarch felt as though he could hear the Harp's heart beating. The grey wood made somehow audible in the dark and falling dimness. He wondered what would come next. He was controlling, but he was not in control.

"As I have said already," she whispered kindly, "you do not know me for you do not know yourself, and you do not know yourself because you do not acknowledge them." She paused, letting her last note linger in the still space between them.

"Them?" he questioned.

"I created all and in that creation all was created. The trees and their flowers, the birds that swim in the rivers, and the birds that swim in the air above the flowing wells, the drifting river Waters. Gills and lungs, scales and feathers, let alone your leathers: all is and was carried when I played my song."

"That is all over now," Macguarch interjected.

"No," the Harp returned apathetically. "The pious know only the paltry side of love, the trivial and the singular. The fearless alone feel her tragedies."

"We are not a pious people," he returned defensively. "Or at least not like that. Balor is the king. That is good enough."

"No, you have made kings into gods. That is worse," she said. "I created by knitting together sinews like lotus silk. A central Kinship, a lifting Oneness. A unifying thread, in my music the world was wed. There are no kings that I recognize."

She straightened herself, freeing her feet from the wonderfully rippled and greying boards below. She looked at him and smiled. A tear welling like a dew drop on the smallest leaf.

"Statutes need statues," he responded, "the moral order of our people comes from kingship and law. Rights."

"No," the Harp returned.

She paused. Breathing a shaman's breath, a pregnant inhale. Then, she let it out. "The notion of a stable cosmological order matched by the priestly concept of a social order governed by kings is the basis not for your society, but your slavery.

"In coming ages and also the ages of your past, the narrow visage of the heavens will shift, have shifted, its aperture and the restricted portions of eternity will grow insular and lonely. By extending, you will bind yourself in. By reaching, you have already fallen."

"By reaching, we have found you," he said, squeezing her body with his great webbed hands even tighter. The ancient greying oak sapped under his fingers, and a pain surged through her limbs.

"And by finding you," he continued, "we have ushered our enslavement of your people into a new culture of colonization. A new and strong religion over your pagan pedagogy." He paused, feeling a holy righteousness surge through his veins. His back straightened, and his eyes, now distended but clear, found new life like a preacher at a podium. "You speak of animism, of life interwoven within all, but what then will become of the clown when the mist of your pagan dream evaporates into the clear of daylight?"

"What is daylight?" the Harp asked.

"It is the absence of night, of course," the Oceaner replied simply.

"No, it is the Sun."

A heavy stillness fell with her words, like the Sun's set. It was pink and yellow. Honor alluring the honorable. An invitation.

But Macguarch's energy sliced through the stillness, and he continued, "The God of the universe is far more generous than the wraith walking your words."

"But are you?"

"Am I what?"

"Generous?"

This time, the silence echoed through the dim darkness. It held firm those actors playing below. His righteous vigor, like all righteous vigor locked in veins, was for his own soul's victory and required no defense. The Oceaners were near their reckoning, a culture organizing to consume themselves from the inside or to cast their teeth outward to find new life—new souls or culture or capital to devour, to feed their righteous appetites.

"The linear pretense, your pretense," the Harp said, pointing her heart into his, "of absolute objectivity rules in favor over majesty, of individuals shining like stars."

"We don't care for stars. We live under the lapping seas."

"You came from the stars," the Harp returned, "and now you drift in the blue deep. The forever dark."

After a pause, a deep salience, one even I could taste in colors of red and burnt yellow, the Harp said, "You may take me. But you will never have me. You have understood me as a petal to adorn your coat, a decoration to charm your vanity, an accouterment of the summer's day. You have come here as an invisible entrant, sneaking into our tents and snaking into my home, but you are not invisible."

Another pause. Another silent prominence.

"But I see you," the Harp whispered.

"And I have you," Macguarch whispered back, chuckling through his lips.

"Yes," she said simply. "You shape nature to suit you. Your righteous anger is for yourself. That is why you are here, and that is why you were, epochs ago, cast under the ocean. A lid has closed over your eyes."

"Your people let nature shape them."

"Yes. To suit all."

"All?" he questioned aggressively.

"All," she answered simply, letting a single tear fall and splash upon the floor. "You may take me. You are already deep into your work. My sermon is over, the words cast and casting still. Let us go."

Harp in hand, Macguarch walked forward to the great door, encumbered only slightly by his prize. He stepped into the growing light and looked east to the reddening dawn.

The village was already deep into their morning, ambling about their fires, but no one saw him. The Moon hung in the sky and conspired with the morning fires to bathe the village in a faint glow.

Two Mothers, one young and the other old, stepped out of their tent, and their feet splashed in unexpected puddles.

Ponds and plains.

Plains in ponds.

The Ocean was walking upon the Land.

The mist abated as the Sun readied to crest.

The cold air warming for its rise.

But the Land was silent.

Her music was gone.

That same morning.

The beams of the long house were sewn of precious Mountain oak that were hewn and shaped by the trees themselves.

The conversation between the Oceaner and the Harp molded in the dark corner of the house like spoiled meat, but the oak beams remembered, they always remembered and held what they saw deep in their cambial sap and ageless marrow.

I thought the long house's architecture was quite attractive. It is not often that villages and their protruding structures blend with the landscape, even during this time of our history. But, this was a fine building for this village was not your often type.

I know a friend who built a home in the rafters at the heart of the cruck blade that runs parallel to the outside walls and the brace that connects the blade to the collar of the roof.

The branch that chose to be the cruck blade was a tired oak. She must have been, for when The People's carpenters put her in place, she cracked and then twisted at the top, revealing a perfect place for a hair nest—human hair, of course, collected when you put it down.

My friend, the bird, raised many young there in the warmth of the twisting oak and fired hearth.

But let me get on with the story.

————

The overstrikes of the axe that land in perpendicular strikes often present in such buildings were lacking throughout the structure—there were no marks to remind the wrights of their imperfection.

"It casts a peculiar Oneness, don't you think?" Miach asked as he placed the herbs on the table and marveled at the perfect architecture of the long house around and above them. This was not his first time in the hall, but its peculiar structure was something that often made him speechless—a recurrent awe.

Those preparing the night's medicines at the other end of the hall smiled and nodded pleasantly.

"What was it like?" Miach asked.

"What was what like?" the herbalists responded.

"The music?" Miach played with his ears.

"Everything," they said solemnly. "It was everything. When you closed your eyes, you could see the ripples of resonance over the meadow. You could hear it float in subtle whites that fell into landed yellows and oranges as they drifted through the crowded woods of the elevated plains, reaching for the Mountain when it played between the trunks of oaks and willows on Cailleach's deepening banks. She created our world. Her music was our world."

"Why did—" Miach asked, fumbling for the words, a faint blush coloring his cheeks. Blood flushed like foxglove.

The Harp's emptiness that stood in the corner of the long house was pungent and painful. He wished, they all did, that he would have noticed her presence in the village before she was gone, before she was taken. He wished he would have stayed there, in the dark of the long house, with closed eyes and open ears, letting her music sift and sort through him. To raise him kindly and let him fall fully, once more, against Earth, against himself.

"They took her in order to take us from ourselves," they said, inferring his question, "to disconnect us from ourselves. Harmony is the most potent force walking this Earth. It is sharper than steel and stronger than tumbling Mountain stone."

"Harmony?" the boy inquired. His eyes were still searching the beams lacing the ceiling.

"Yes, it carries like the river Cailleach's current, and it unites and weaves and connects and attunes the many into the One. And when the One stands, woven and brocaded in sinew and stone, in blood and bone, nothing can oppose it. No one can oppose us."

The herbalists' words ricocheted through his heart-mind, a thought welling like putrid water but aromatic like meadow flowers. Both alien and homely—a truth that was true but felt momentarily false.

The herbalists worked the herbs and flowers into the table without looking up, and the silence skittered about the rafters until its weight accumulated and crashed down like particles in precipitation.

"They took it to separate themselves from the Land," the herbalists continued, muttering momentarily and then falling silently into their work.

———————

Miach could just catch the gleam of the wax-covered compound leaves of the Ash outside of the house. Her tremulous arms emitted from the diamond-furrowed bark opposite of each other, like human arms. They seemed hardly capable of bearing the burden of beauty, their grandeur. Her branches waving in the valley's wind.

Now and then, a fantastic meander of curlews sprung from the bogs below and flew into the Ash, stretching their long diaphanous silk drapes and producing a subtle reprieve and slight shadow show upon the house.

But no music waved in the trees. No melody was heard in the bogs below. The Land was broken and broken apart. The plain mourned its mother.

————

The herbalists worked within the long house and upon the furniture constructed during The Two Fires Ceremony, nearly fifteen thousand years ago. The salmon-white beams and herb-beaten tables only recently turning grey, youth still creaking as it settled.

The architect was the first Mother, the Ancient One. It is said that she carried the *Fáil* Stone from *Falias* that now rests atop the bald Mountain and the great *Sled* that rests above the hearth—its javelin-like shaft with tipped iron reflecting the winter's fire into the hall and lighting the space with great silver light.

The herbalists worked atop the tables, and they worked in silence. The floor was littered with shavings and fibrous stems that their naked feet steadily ground into a stringy pulp. Ropes and medicine to weave. Hand and foot ready for the tasks.

Their efforts pulsed a purposed energy, every moment weighed lightly, but every moment dedicated to some end. Their gentle fingers plucked leaf from stem as the Horse sifts for soft grass with her upper lip. They were careful but quick and well-practiced in this sacred Art. The spine and apical of every leaf left in perfect form.

"Handle them well," one would remind another.

And, "Yes, thank you, sister."

And, "Soft, we become the tie of leaf to stem."

And, "Each spine, every apical a Caldron that must stay closed," another would remind back, generally and most often from the lips of the oldest.

Bundles of herbs crackled in the rafters above their oily hair when the valley's air filtered through the open door, carrying an admixture of tan and teal—dust lingering on the backs of grass and Water.

There were brews of *Brigid-root*, for bitterness and its cleansing truth for digestion, *Strewing-leaf*, for edging the dead onward, and *Self-Heal*, for cleansing the heart-speak and freeing the stilled voices. Each bundle, each brew, drying above them. On the table, powders in mortars overflowed into ochre ampoules, and bales of wilted leaves were tied into smudges. One bale smoked in the corner, dripping a grey and precious pollution upward.

"Juniper," Miach whispered as his lips tasted the perfume. "A grey flume whitening into a thin veil," he said as he approached the table. "The Otherworld—why is it so close?"

The herbalists, who were called The Children of Cécht, the weavers of power, worked silently in their medicine. They were braiding rue for listening, sage for swelling, vervain for spirit, and wort for dreaming into plaited bundles wrapped with the green sinew of the rowan tree. They would suck and chew on the bark, the astringent, zinc, and iron life visiting their palate. Then, when its rigid structure became moist and bendable, they would wrap it around the bale that was held by their hands.

"The Mothers held a vision," one of The Children, a Salmon, responded without looking up and after taking a strip of bark out of her mouth.

"Yes, I saw the clouds this morning," Miach said.

The Salmon's hands paused, her eyes now swimming in the grey and white smoke to Miach. She hesitated, holding the boy's last words.

"Our trees and rivers are not in season. Earth is out of her pace. My memory is feeble in this torrent. My body is lost in this current." At this, she placed another strip of peeling rowan bark in her mouth and looked down, continuing the plait with drawn fingers.

"The Mothers saw the Ocean walk into the sky this morning," another of The Children replied, but to no one particularly.

"Over the lone Mountain in a cresting yellow mist, if I heard it right," another tacked on.

"A very unnatural business," the last of The Children, a Ring Ouzel, said when her mouth became free from her work.

She was the newest inculcate of The Children and a beautiful bird with a white breastplate. She had recently traveled across the oceanland, and she was here to breed but offered her services in the long house while she waited.

She would speak no more than what she had said.

Miach looked at the Salmon, and his eyes glinted. He scanned over to the Ouzel, and a tear welled and then fell down to his lips. It steamed to join their smoke.

"I have learned much, I have seen much and walked with many. I have touched and shared with valleys and lowland hills, and my roots have yawned deeper into the bottomless clay than most. But," he paused, playing with the words and the strange salt their evaporation left behind, "I have never seen this."

The Children steadied in their medicine. The smoke filtered up and out of the open doorway and created new clouds above the village. Dark clouds. Rain clouds that threatened a great storm. A deluge.

"The Old Mother asked for moon-water," The Children said together. "It has something to do with these omens. But we will need the mugwort."

"I understand," the boy, the medicine man, returned. "We will go."

———————

It did not take long for the brothers to prepare for their journey. They did not need much. They never did.

Miach would harvest roots for food as they walked, and Long-Arm knew the land well, for his play with Pryderi often flirted with the boundary that kissed the scared uplands to the south. What was a few more steps, a few strides higher into the Land of light and fire, of rising stone and tumbling winds?

That is where the finest patch of mugwort grew, they knew, for she had told them (the mugwort) during a winter fire many years ago. Flames lapped the hearth's stone like a dog on a hot day. They danced as the wood gave way. The People were rapt by her story and stage. She smiled and cried when she spoke of this place—the place high upon the Mountain that was now lost in memory but found in love, maybe.

Later that morning, the brothers left. They put the village at their backs and walked into the rocky hills. They journeyed until the day became evening and then walked even further as they watched the evening fall into the dusking dark. They camped under the star-lit sky when the Moon was high. Miach cast himself on the ground and fell asleep at once, for slumber had evaded him for many nights. But, there was something about the clear Mountain air that soothed him into a deep slumber. Something calm and comforting. Something natural.

The brothers dreamed of breakfast.

It happened before dawn was in the sky that Long-Arm woke and rose. Miach was still deep in sleep, but the cold refreshed Long-Arm and shook him awake. He gazed eastward into the running dawn's darkness as pensive and silent as a tree on a windless night. The grey of night retreating before the pale pink crest of red and orange, of the Sun and his light.

"Darkness is not the absence of light," he remembered Pryderi telling him as they ventured deep into the plain beyond the village many years ago, "but that which runs when the light becomes."

Images and memories of their first trip deep into the eastern edge of the plain floated around his eyes like parietal cave art, and he smelled the flowers and summer grasses waft and play with the soft hairs in his nose. Pryderi did not speak about the Sun and light often. She frequently told other stories of olden days and heroes and gods in gardens that walked with them. Her stories were of rising and falling, her characters always brave, always knowing what to do and how to act. But he was not brave, or so he thought, and he was never sure as to what he should do.

"Becomes what?" he remembered asking her, a memory of him kneeling astride a curlew nest that lay above the stream arose in the morning mist around him.

"You," she nickered in response.

He smiled back, unsure.

It was not long until Miach was awake and crested his limbs into a stretch, twisting his hands this way and that, revealing the white of his palms.

"Ah, you're awake," Long-Arm said when his brother's motion caused his gaze to fall back on the camp.

"My very bones are chilled," Miach said, flapping his wrists and stamping his feet, trying to move the blood. It had turned cold in the night, and the dawn played with becoming even colder. The sky was a bleak and charmless blue.

The day was yet young under the eastern shadow, and a frost fought life into a white stillness. From their vantage, the brothers could see the tall grasses lacing the plain fading fast into autumn gold. They could see the water pooling in the low spots, the grasses drowning, gold or otherwise. All becoming a pallid black and deep blue, soon.

The village far below was yellowing and seemed to burn as the Sun reflected against her glowing chimneys of smoking bacon and eggs. Smokeholes threw smoke that soon fell away and sailed off in shaggy dragging strings. The Sun glistened unnaturally upon the plain, reflecting against a new and growing glass surface.

The brothers had only just begun their breakfast of roots cooked over heated stones when the growing light worked to kick them on.

"If only that smell would waft up here in nibbles of blackened sweet fat," Long-Arm said, his words breaking the still concentration of his brother.

"I would be happier if we could find some curly or even yellow dock," Miach said to himself. His heart scanned the landscape around them. "Nothing but grey here," he thought.

"Yes, only rocks here, it seems," the younger brother spit between bites of the roots. "I have left you some. Here," he said with an outflung arm tipped by the dull spearhead of the red clay plate, "they taste almost as good as they did last night. I thought about not leaving you any."

"Only sharp rocks and grey Earth," Miach responded without noticing the plate shoved in his face. "We must get higher. Above this." The invitation of burnt roots was unvictorious.

"Why would that make you happy?" Long-Arm returned, kicking a stone and watching it run downhill. Run, he thought to himself. "There is little as good as that—" he said out loud, interrupting his own question.

"—As what?" Miach asked impatiently.

"Sorry," he smirked. "What about dock? I don't particularly enjoy the taste."

"Mother said that she once lived up here, beyond the dock. Or, maybe I am dreaming," Miach said.

Long-Arm smirked a short smile in response and echoed a soundless but stringent respiration in Miach's direction. He did not remember that story. But he trusted that Miach did. And so he smiled.

They packed their camp and set out.

At first, they fought a low thicket of cedar, a burgeoning savanna, really, just not yet, and they climbed higher, pushing through the brambles and nettle patches that had sprung up like gophers. They then pushed their way through a dense copse of deciduous trees, and then, once through the copse of trees, they fell into a stone land that lay beyond. The brothers squeezed close, hands touching when they must, breath tickling little hairs and little leaves alike. Short strong branches ripped at their shoulders, and so they squeezed closer, tighter, like two babes in the womb.

Eventually, but not long, Long-Arm and Miach's exploration fell, as I said, into an open stone space beyond the small forest. They moved gently across the timeless landscape, shoved on by spirits and ghosts and travelers past. The clearing was spacious but not special. It was a world greying under stone, like the Land that they had traversed all morning, but peculiar.

There was a void that called to them. Some emptiness that asked for filling.

This is what pulled them.

A silent storm rumbled beyond the Rim in the distance and shook the Mountain with every thunderous roar or lightning strike—the brothers did not know which, for it was beyond the Rim, and they could not see it.

Miach stumbled when his foot met a loose stone, and he tumbled a few strides down the hill.

"Are you okay?" Long-Arm asked, stretching out his long arm to help him back up.

It was too late. Miach was already up, standing on his feet with a small trickle of blood, a trifle really, crusting through his pants below the knee. Miach's eyes were warm, and they looked about the landscape, smelling something particular.

"Are we there?" Long-Arm inquired, leaning in but pulling his arm back.

"Not here," Miach said. His wide eyes scything through the open space of grey and greying stone. "But she knows we are coming. She feels us."

"The storm seems to be getting worse the higher we go."

"We are getting closer with every step," Miach returned. "The storm will not touch us. She flicked it on to slow us down. Not to harm us."

"Why?" Long-Arm asked, his fears mounting like tumbling stone.

"She needs a moment."

"A moment? What is a moment to her?"

"A lumber lurching, a bee bumbling, a boy blundering his knee on stone," Miach said. "Everyone needs a moment."

———————

It required some time to scale the immense truncated walls of sloping stone, to negotiate the hillside, and cross the borderland between the rising valley and the Mountain mist.

They walked steadily on. They traced the lay line of the Mountain that cut across her face from the valley to the Rim of their world. It wound always more down than up, but the brothers continued until they rose higher.

"Altitude is a strange thing, don't you think?" Miach asked.

"I feel its form. Is that what you mean?" Long-Arm returned, himself now stumbling over a jagged and loose stone. He struggled to catch his breath.

"Yes, I guess." Miach's eyes questioned the landscape into a deeper inquiry. "I feel her stones becoming less smooth, less rounded by the Waters. And yet," he continued, "I feel more grounded the higher we go. There is a peculiar aloneness here that is calling into me. No," he paused, feeling the winds waving his fingers and twisting them from green to white, "a void wanting found."

The brothers approached a deep Mountain valley surrounded by the upland and loose copse of Rowan and Alder. A lone stunted tree, distorted by the constant pull of the place, was bent in a caricature of arrested motion. An eternal prayer, a held pallor of the petulant and moody silver wind.

The Rowan and Alder had vanished many years ago from the lower lands and moist watersheds when the Ancient One sent fire into the Mountain. A community of mutualism, the Green Alder sprouting when the Red Rowan burns and the Red Rowan becoming bushy for the Stag to browse when the Alder calls the lightning in.

The bones of their abode ashen and happy.

"Blood rusting down when their bones rise into dust," Miach said, handing the blackened charcoal that he had only just picked up to his brother, who placed it gently on his tongue. Long-Arm let the many pores dissipate the peculiar memory. It steamed and sizzled on his palate, and then it powdered into an ancestral lingua.

Smacking his lips, he puckered and pointed down the trail. "We are close—she tastes like we are close," Long-Arm said, "She says to keep walking."

In front of them, but a little higher, the Mountain's upland valley bulked silently below an escarpment of stone that punctuated the cliff face—what The People called the *Snechtai*, or The Snow, for the outcropping was clad in white marble and reflected the Sun's light like a lighthouse over the plain. When the Rowan and Alder burned below the *Snechtai*, a red haze reflected across the Land. Like the Sun's rise, but different.

It was not long before Miach found the signs he was looking for. They first lay on the borders of the last Alder grove and then again lived in small patches under the engorged bowl of the hidden valley.

"She was here not long ago," he said with searching eyes, his knees bending as he fell into a squat.

The Land around them was well-drained, rocky, and held black soils kissed by lightning—a Land that flashed white and then settled ungently under a duvet of red flame that found herself as a winking orange ember that fell, slowly and finally, into her black and Stygian grave. A grave becoming a cradle, death burning life anew.
Today, she was green. The brothers walked on. Their heads hunched with scything eyes.

"And how do you suppose she got here?" asked Long-Arm.

"I do not know for sure, of course, but I dream that the fire's tremendous updraft pulled her into a rich ascent," Miach returned, his eyes tasting the landscape.

"Or maybe she ran up here to taste the wind?" Long-Arm reasoned, thinking selfishly. "Or perhaps she ran up here to be the wind."

The brothers smiled at each other and their shared Kinship. They walked on.

As they did, Long-Arm mentioned, "She once told me that some *want* change. Others want *to* change. And yet, there are those who are the change." He whinnied a laugh, thinking of the wind that was playing about them.

"Great abbreviators we are," Miach responded, laughing back. "We touch what we know, and we are touched by that which is, in great part, us. But we don't see all because we are not all, but contained in the all and there, within the all, we all are—well, all." His face stammered the confusion of his words with flaccidity.

"Mugwort lives this change," Long-Arm said, grounding the

subject to his liking. He was altogether unsure about what his brother was getting at.

Soon, it happened that their eyes landed, together, on a curled and yellowing leaf of dock and then many more not twenty yards in front of them. Blood-red javelins thrust through the morning frost and carried little red bulbs of adorned white hearts. Their leaves spiked as they twisted and invited the brother onward.

Seeing the signs, they stepped carefully now.

"Where there is community, there also may I be," Miach said, uttering a map given to him at birth. "Find first the community, attuning to our music, and there you will find me, a note surrounded by many others," the mugwort's words floating about them now like liquors of smoke.

The brothers continued on, meandering across and up the Mountain, stepping over the scorched Earth with solemnity.

Soon, the Mountain's once rocky surface changed. The land that lay before them became accented by a lush red-green carpet. Her carpet. She grew with spears on feathery stems, and they could smell her pungency many steps downwind. The mugwort's words continued to float about them, a memory colored by releasing frost, a morning steam growing legs and walking with them. It comforted them, Miach more so, and stilled any fears.

"Be fearless," she long ago told Miach, "as though you walk in dreams."

"I have courage," Miach thought out loud. His hands picked and then uncurled her leaves between his thumb and forefinger and burled the dust with the morning dew.

"No, fearless, like dreams," she asserted back both in memory and also the reality that floated at their feet.

Kneeling with the red and green and white, the brothers sifted through curled leaves and harvested the mugwort's medicine. She smiled at the brothers as Long-Arm twisted his satchel to his belly, and Miach offered a prayer.

They harvested the morning long and laughed, fearlessly.

———————

Soon, a handful of pungent leaves littered their satchels full, and they began their descent downhill back to the village to deliver their collection to The Children of Cécht for the moon-water. The smoking chimneys of the village were now a downdraft pulling their rich descent.

The village was wide awake now, groaning as all old villages do at the end of a long night. Settling into endless days and balancing the endlessness of their days with the infiniteness of their ways.

As their journey fell, Long-Arm thought he saw the color of a girl trail behind a stone outcropping. It was hard to tell. The morning's Mountain mist was descending with them, but it covered some distance below. It was moving less spiritedly and was taking its time.

A dance of coral pink fluttered into an orchid twirl before his eyes could refocus.

"Did you see that?" he snapped, grabbing his brother's forearm.

"See what?" Miach responded.

"That—" Long-Arm pointed spiritedly at the color as it resurfaced with a flicker from behind another large stone topped with mist. It, whatever it was, then vanished as swiftly as it had come.

"No mind!" Miach said aggressively. "We have to get back, The Children are waiting—"

"Hold on—I have to—let me look," the younger brother said, already departing from the path.

He closed the distance in a few strides, and he quickly rounded the large stone's corner. The road was rough and broken, moss fading over stone, and an old winding footpath was covered under a thick carpet of campion flowers. White sedum crested over the west-facing rocks like sun-kissed fingers waving and riding atop roseroot and sandwort. White purling pink into a knit and colorful blanket.

Saxifrage, her leaves like little hands holding the heart of the Mountain, had cleft a rock in half to his left. And so he kept to the right out of fear or respect. Then, his steps awakened into a perfectly grey and unhewn stone enclosure. A living dolmen waiting for rebirth.

His eyes moved, and his head searched, but to his dismay, neither pink nor coral was to be found.

The girl was gone.

Only a ghost stepping the dew down. The mist floated longer than its friends. It was held by some magnetic incongruity within the Mountain and was strangely both energized by a center stone and chained to it.

He could but hold his breath.

The place spoke a peculiar sacredness.

He looked around the escarpment and the center stone that was shrouded in mist.

He was alone.

Miach had disappeared, and even the Sun stopped His rising. Long-Arm's endless pulsing and babbling with his brother stilled in his heart as the mist shrouded around him. Thought fell downward as the mist floated up. He felt it wave through him.

Then, a strange and rusting chain secured his feet in place. It ripped from the cleft stone that was now behind him and belched the twisted iron shackles from the Underworld. It tightened like a Raven's claw around his ankles, sinking its steel talons into his skin.

He could not move.

He was alone.

Or so he thought.

A dreariness fell upon him, and he nodded, nearly napping. Suddenly, there came a tapping.

————————

"Hello," a lone feminine voice resounded against the circle of stones like a whisper in an otherwise empty room.

The boy's eyes became awake and peered a quick pace through the white mist. A reawakened energy beat through him. But he saw no one.

"Long-Arm." Again, her voice.

Then, silence.

Nothing but mist on stone.

The boy looking.

No one.

He was alone.

No. I was here.

————————

A peculiar ache settled from his legs upward like those who lay for too long and need to stretch. He tried to arch his back, to throw his arms above his head, to unfurl his clutched fingers. But nothing moved.

Some strange Art penetrated and locked him in a hypnotic stupor.

I giggled a gurgling croak at his feeble attempt.
I did, I have to admit it.
I admired his desire to break my power.

"Have I been dreaming?" the boy's heart pounded. "How long have I been here?" his mind questioned, tepidly, as though he did not really want the second question answered.

It was not until he was long into the moment that Long-Arm

realized where he was. The mist abated just enough for him to see that the stones at his feet were cut and shaped around the center of the space. A masterful craftsmanship mixed with the coarse jaggedness of the stone hollow that towered above him. Memories, certain stories, bubbled up his throat. They danced on his lips.

The strange mist veiled the circular space and partially covered the center stone's surface. A light filtered through the shroud, and it played like children on the Mountain stones. It jumped from this to that with giggles that streamed all around. A loving sound carried in the strained and tiring laughter of too long a respire.

After some time, even the Mountain morning's ghost floated her way and left with the children at play. A cleansed and silver clarity took its place, like a sunrise that was late but still was. The silver transformed into a yellowish-red as the center stone revealed itself.

You will one day say they were rocks.
They maintain that they are old trees.
I believe the rocks.

"The *Fáil* stone," he whispered forcefully to himself when he saw its face.

He had never been here before, for the last Mother's coronation was before his time, but his body knew this place well. A Mountain itself, the *Fáil* stone was the vision stone, the phallic symbol of their people. It was where their leaders, The Mothers, were coronated on the summer's solstice, where ceremony broke the long winter and dawdling spring.

"We have lived long in this deep winter of our people," he remembered Pryderi telling him one day as they ran together along the river Cailleach. They had stopped to rest under the grove of white willow, and she told him many things.

"Long ago, the *Fáil* stone was the rite of our people, a seasonal dispatch of the dead and a coronation of the new running and flying and growing and crawling and swimming amongst us." Her words floated through him like memories untethered by color and taste.

"Under its feet, the Stag were born. Atop its tip, the Sun crests every morning—if we sing, when we sing. This is why we sing. To create the world every morning," she said, smiling. Long-Arm loved her smile like a mother loves the soft cooing lips of the lapping babe.

"But not today." Pryderi's words continued to play through him, a distant echo, an internal heart-pulse. "They have replaced our kind with kings."

At this, he fell from the memory dream with a snap and looked around him. The red began overtaking the yellow of the stone circle, his bloodshot eyes pooling as his blood boiled upward, releasing a single tear. It trickled silently down. The memories were gone, floating away like the mist, Pryderi running, even in dream.

The Oceaners took many things from them, not the least of which was the power of their dreams.

"Rebirth," Long-Arm said to himself, his attention snapping to his surroundings like hooves on brittle oak branches. His eyes rotated, and his heart kneeled at the stone's base. Skintight images floated amongst him in flashes of white and red—of song and sacrifice. He lifted his hands as though to grab them, but he strangled the thin air with the worthlessness of empty and closed palms. He tried to touch the visions, but they evaded him.

Instead, they landed on the stone like splattered paint.

He blinked when they flaunted their color against the grey and marbled white, and he saw the days of old written in stories and symbols. Blood. Blood was the ink of choice.

Stag with necks cut and life welling in frothy beads. Bison harvesting men. Men with spears thrust through the bison's abdomen, and their entrails leaking downward. A bird on a staff. Shamans they were. Herds of Horses running the dust down, tornadoes at their feet recasting Earth's flat form into something fonder. A chaos of human hands, stained in red and with a few fingers truncated midway—from the long winters past but also from the summers of use. The lone pregnant Horse, belly swelling into white, the carrier of man, her mane yellowing into gold. These stories were etched into the stone. Long ago.

"Rebirth," he again said, this time loud enough for his ears to hear, acknowledging the sacredness of this place.

"I am rebirth," he continued, in the practiced way. "I am blood and bone and soon I am the Waters rusting as I slither over flame and stone. I am Water reborn in blood."

The words floated through him from places hitherto unknown. The power of the place pulled them out. Memories becoming tasted thoughts, drawn on clean sheets of vellum. At this, his ache settled and stilled, and he was awash in the mist and loosed in her cleansing torrent.

He had hardly spoken these words when there came a great drumming and rolling *boom* that seemed to erupt from the stone herself. His bones recognized the deep drums, the arcane mineral-rich song of death. It was a sound the Síraide had not heard for many years. On Winter's Eve, they would dance to this drumming and rolling song. They would stomp their feet to its rhythm. This earthen beat, itself telling time what to be. But not as of late, not recently.

"They have replaced our kind with kings," Pryderi's words drifted once again through his heart and this time purled across his lips like storm-borne river waves.

At this, as though kicked into motion by the memory, the boy jumped to his feet in alarm and felt his body return to him as the stones pierced his bare soles. The surge of pain worked from the ground up and awakened something otherwise slumbering in his chest. He tried to walk forward and found himself surprised that the chain was gone.

"Was it ever really there?" he thought.

He stumbled another step across the open space, heart pounding like the loudest drum, barefoot and unclad, his clothes soaked and clinging. The thunder that was once distant rumbled into a drumming conscious roar, a bear bursting irritably from hibernation, and close. The lightning fell in a flash and flickered around him like a broken lamp littering oil. He looked up at the sky and then once more upon the stone.

He had seen lightning before and watched it crest the Rim of the world as the rains followed with their flowing. But this time, it seemed to burn the world in blinking light, a strobed visibility, a broiling might. In each flicker, he could see a circle of stones encasing him. In each flicker, the circle growing smaller. Each flicker, encasing him.

It writhed and went, his view of the stones, the space, coming and going and growing smaller in a burning blue-yellow flame.

Then, true blackness, the absence of light.

He blinked.

The lightning was gone.

He blinked again.

The light of the afternoon grew once more behind the pursed clouds that waved slowly into the clearing sky.

He blinked again, rubbing his eyes this time.

At first, he could see nothing but the leaving mist and etched stone, the ancient images and carpets of flowers and their stone-breaking leaves now hiding below it all.

He placed his open palm upon the stone. His legs ached with acid and were weak. His fingers trembled and shook. The startling realization and memory of this place poured through him, slowly but painfully.

"Hello," again uttered a feminine voice, but this time with the full depth of speech.

He peeled his hand from the stone and spun, searching for the speaker. Slowly, he saw forms encircling the center stone mirrored in a profound black, their tails like peaks and plumes of black flame above the mist. They were glinting stars that glittered yet in the morning sky and were strangely steered by the shadowless figures circling above.

He did not know what to do.

He felt unheroic.

And so he kneeled before the stone.

"Up, my friend," the lone voice smoothly contended. "Up," she said again.

At that, the many black figures circling above like stars solidified with a silvery snap into a lone bird that was perched atop the *Fáil* stone.

I looked upon him.
He looked upon a Raven.

—————————

"Hello," I said.

The boy shifted and cleaned his eyes and then peered deeply into mine with intense attraction. Legs like jelly, he leaned back from a kneel and sat down, crossing his legs and collapsing into the position of ceremony. He did not know what else to do.

"How did you know my name?" he asked.

"What does that matter?" I responded kindly.

"What about my brother?"

"What about him?" my response, again, was kind.

"Where is he? How long have I been here?" he asked.

"These are not your *real* questions, surely," I said with a blank stare. "What is your real question?"

This time, my voice was neither kind nor otherwise. My head twisted so that my deep black eye became fully his. I, the red-mouthed sharp-beaked scald-crow, centered on him.

The mist returned gently, for I called her back, and she settled around us. The stone grumbled under our feet, and a white encrusted yellow flower of the saxifrage emerged in front of him.

"Fresh, it relieves paralysis of the tongue," I giggled an exhale without removing my eye from him. "Eat and then ask your *real* question."

He ate and thanked me.

"We fell from the stars," I continued. "A fine question."

He never asked, but I knew.

"Pryderi told me I fell from her yellowing mane," he said, struggling to keep the smirk from his lips.

I saw his struggle. The saxifrage flower working comically in him. It filled his cheeks and welled into an obvious red.

"Yes, from the stars," I continued. "Our world is the harmony of light and dark, of stars and space, of winter and then summer. Day and her night." I twisted my head and looked elsewhere. "The Sun is a star, and we splashed down when he rose to the music."

"Our star!" the boy responded strongly, looking upward beyond the mist to find the familiar and yellowing white light.

"No," I responded kindly, "a star. It is upon harmony and not title that the battlefield depends."

"What battlefield?" his confusion snapped. "What do *you* mean?"

"What do you mean?" I asked immediately. "Pick a question." My eye again centered on him.

Long-Arm's heart pivoted uncomfortably. His eyes scythed through the hollow and found the cut stones around his feet. Their polished surfaces reflecting the light of a star.

After a long pause, he asked, "Then, what is harmony?"

"Ah!" my voice crackled with a happy, gurgling croak. It tingled in my throat the way we like. "That is a good question. I am glad that you found it." I inhaled deeply. Letting it out, I said, "Harmony is resonance in motion."

"Okay—" he said irritably.

"Harmony is when resonance reincarnates particular truths into universal significance." I ambled a few steps to the west ridge of the stone. It was cooler there. I paused, my feet playing with the stone's icy surface, and I placed my wing over my beak. Thinking. "No, metamorphosizes is a better word than reincarnates."

"Why?" the boy asked. His curiosity was spurred by an unknown but not unwanted dedication to the moment.

"Reincarnation requires death. Metamorphosis requires only acknowledgment and resonance," I said. "Characters have resonance, objects have resonance, colors even have resonance. Life and her moments explore harmony when life and her moments resonate with each other." I laughed again, my head leaning back as I croaked.

"When they acknowledge each other?" he asked, fumbling his fingers in the air. "Is that right? Is that what you mean?"

"Yes," I responded, "to a degree." My head fell back down to him, and a smile crested to weave the space between us with a yellowing light.

"The smallest seeds," I continued, "woven into the fabric of life, awaken their own imaginative world when they become known together."

"Seeds grow in Earth," he said. "What does this have to do with stars?"

"Harmony you asked about," I said sharply, becoming irritable. "The seed and her Earth's own imaginative world awaken when they become known together," I continued, repeating myself. "'The old stories are not effective' and 'we need a new kind of spiritual and social leadership,' your kind whispers under your ornate tapestries woven of cambial threads," I continued, pointing to the village of tents on the valley's floor.

"Warp and what?" he questioned.

"Warp, the threads running lengthwise overcome by the weft, the threads running vertically—the stitches of tapestries and the Music's stitches over the Land are made of warp and weft woven threads. Civilization and its cathedrals, to some degree, are the domination of the weft over the warp. Only the sacred is vertical. The vile is level."

"I guess I am not following," he said, shifting his position and beginning to stand up. "You lost me."

"You lost you," I said, smiling. "This is your story, not mine."

The boy fell back down, pushed by some unknown force in the mist.

At this, the Raven continued, "This has nothing to do with me. I am a teller of story, a trickster in the mist. Will you listen, or will you leave?"

"I will listen," Long-Arm returned apologetically, returning his attention back to the stone.

"And so warp and weft," I continued. "Horizontal, this is your frenetically aggressive creation and consumption of industry and pleasure for the search of either profit or place."

"Industry?" the boy asked, twisting his face.

"Patience, you will see," I returned. "They search for profit and place, as I said. Profit in the sense that there is nothing left for them to attain or conquer other than more of the same, and place in the sense that, to attain the first, they must heighten their location in the field of command. The battlefield, remember?"

"I remember, but what about harmony?" he returned.

"The air is free, and so you do not protect it. The land under your feet is not, and so you do. But, if you were to lose only one of Earth's gifts, air or land, what would you choose?" I asked.

"Why do I have to choose?" he inquired. A peculiar urgency in his voice, a fervor hitherto lacking.

"They are coming, and you, all of you," I motioned again to the valley, "must soon choose."

"Choose what?" he asked.

"They leave no room for heretics who talk to land and not landowners. Those uncommitted to incumbency, those untethered to tenure."

"Tenure?" the boy asked.

"Ownership is their story. Settlement is their music's theme. If we need a new story to rise up and save us, then we need the heretic's old story."

"What story?" Long-Arm asked.

"The story of seed and Earth, of fruit and its womb," I returned, a smile once again cresting upon my beak. "The seed and her Earth's own imaginative world awaken when they become known together, do you recall?" I asked.

"Yes, I remember," he returned.

"They awaken when you acknowledge and then attend to their relationship."

"Yes, regardless of whether we know this particular seed or its Earth or not, like a metaphor," he returned, confidently growing his words into strength.

"That is right—the living metaphor, animism, is the generative force of harmony and its resonance."

"Okay—I am not following," his embarrassment welling to replace any surety he had gained. "What is the difference between harmony and resonance?"

"Another fine question—" I said, tasting the answer like ripe red berries. I walked back to the east end of the stone.

"Thank you," he said with recovering confidence. "I guess, then, I also want to know what harmony and resonance has to do with brocaded sinews of warp and weft weaves and seeds and such."

"Harmony is resonance in motion, as I have said, but we can see harmony as the seed's relationship with her Earth, while resonance is our acknowledgment of their collective matrimony."

"So harmony is particular, and resonance is universal?" he asked.

"Yes, well, that is fine enough for now," I said, pivoting on the rock and fluffing the morning from my feathers. "Resonance is acknowledged harmony."

"Let me work this straight." His fingers twirled the mist in the air, and his eyes stared at the white circles washing from their motion. "You are saying that harmony is relationship, it is the warp threads running lengthwise. It is particular truths known personally. It is community. It is Kinship."

"Yes, good," I returned, holding space.

"Resonance is acknowledgment," he continued. "It is the weft threads running vertically. It is the personal ushered into the heavens, into the universal. A note tuning all. It is communion. It is Oneship."

"Yes, good," I returned. The space becoming full.

"Harmony is Kinship. Resonance is Oneship," he said with growing confidence. "Through Kinship, we have Oneship. That is what you mean by harmony is resonance in motion?" he asked.

"Yes, very good," I returned, smiling.

"And so it is this. Harmony connects us with each other. Resonance, acknowledging that relationship, threads us to the divine, to the gods."

I giggled a diaphonic gurgle. "That is good, I think. I like that. It tastes right and well-seasoned, like rotting offal."

"If that is harmony and metamorphosis and all the like," he said, waving his hands again in a rolling motion to indicate that there was more to say, "then what is the battlefield?"

His question was sure and strong, lacking the dimness of earlier. He leaned back, placing his hands behind him. Then, after a long silence, he asked, "And what about stars?"

"A star feels their way through the darkness," I said, lifting my wings into a full spread, the mist once again ascending in a stark white against my blue sheened black feathers.

"Okay," he responded incuriously but leaning forward into the stone as if his ears were the problem.

"A star is memory carried over fire and colored by flame," I returned.

"So a star is story?"

"Yes, don't you think?"

"I try not to think," he said, remembering Pryderi's teachings about thinking with his head and feeling with his heart-mind.

"Stories are tapestry's finely woven," I said.

"Ah!" he exclaimed. "Yes, both horizontal and vertical, a linen of Kinship and Oneship."

"Yes, they are most alive in fire," I said, leaning into him under a rugged and pregnant silence. I stared into him. I let the words hang and dissipate. Then, looking even deeper, I said, "Prepare for fire."

At this, a grey gust of wind threw the boy backward, and he awoke in front of the stone. He was alone. The mist was burned off even the northern faces of the jagged escarpment, and the Sun had already crested over the Mountain that towered high above him.

I was gone.

My mist left with me.

"Long-Arm!" A lone voice beamed and then echoed against the now unimposing grey around him.

Miach's voice fluttered uphill, his right hand waving above his head and his head turning to look below to the valley.

"Don't tarry, or we will miss tonight's fire." Miach paused, turning around. "The Mothers asked everyone to be there."

Long-Arm backed away from the great stone and turned to rejoin his brother. He was unsure what was real and what was not. Walking away, a few strides now downhill, he turned his head to look upon the stone and its black bird one last time. One last check.

Neither were there. Loose Mountain stones tumbled at his feet, nothing more.

"How long were you calling me?" Long-Arm asked his brother.

"How long what?" Miach responded. "I only called the once."

The brothers walked down, together, one behind the other, to the village. Long-Arm never replied. And he thought it was better that way—left liminal at confusion. A short smile crested on his lips, a small exhale squeezing through.

In the valley, they splashed lightly through deepening puddles. The smell of moistened manure was now sharp in the air. It was early afternoon when they arrived at the long house with the Mountain's mugwort.

That same morning, but a
world away.

Are you sure this is Harmonizes Us to All Things?" Balor, the one-eyed king of the Oceaners, questioned.

"Yes," Macguarch replied. The Harp's strange conversation lingered in the darkness that lay like heavy smoke in his chest.

"My smiths are ready, I am told. Their fires blaze the forge's fervor. She may have created their world in a musical fire, but today, we will destroy it in a songless flame."

"My king, are you sure—"

"Destroy it!" Balor screamed, slamming his fist against the throne below him. It was crafted in silver and sea pearls that his grandfather, many ages ago, welded within the great seamount that towered above the throne room.

"Without it," Balor continued, "the Síraide are like the tongue of the Cormorant: songless and without power. Without the Harp, they are worthless. We will show those wood worshiping Children what

Kinship truly means..."

The king's words trailed off as his attention fell to his lap. His hands were crossed at his waist, and a thumb-ring's shadow lingered emptily on his finger.

"Today is the day for burning. Tomorrow, our waters will crest over the plain," he said without looking up.

"My king," Macguarch said after a brief pause. "Her words, they worry me. She said that we will never *have* her. I did not understand, I do not still—what she meant. She said we shape nature to suit ourselves. That we—"

"—We destroy!" The king shot out of his throne faster than his words could fill the void, and he fell upon Macguarch's neck, fingers turning white as they puddled and played with the red in the chieftain's veins. He sunk his fingers deep into the thick neck of the Harp's thief, and a rush of carmine air rolled like an ebullient carpet through the king's chamber.

The chieftain shrieked a guttural wail, a sound waving from an unfathomable agony that was choked, ultimately, by the welling blood.

Then, the white foam of the deep sea water crested behind the reddening breeze and admixed rudely with Macguarch's spurting blood into a thick coagulated jelly. The Harp's thief lay motionless on the stone floor. Only in his leg was there still movement, still a sliver of life, the spasmodic twitch of mortis.

"Take him away," the king said, standing up and falling back upon his throne. He licked the blood from under his nails.

His plan was well into motion, the pieces were set, the hate finally finding its place. There was no time for doubt. No room for the doubter.

He waved with a discordant flick of his wrists, and attendants fell from the walls and dragged the stiff corpse over the stone floor, leaving a trail of crusting red salt behind.

Then, pointing to the Harp that sat silently and now alone in the room, Balor said, "Take it. Burn it. Tell me when it is done and she is gone."

He then inhaled an unnatural pause, a distended pregnant swell. The room shifted. A tsunami of faltering and flashing light sparked quivering rays of light from the walls of the very room itself, the walls shaking the evil loose.

"Prepare the men and sharpen the steel," Balor continued. "We leave at dawn."

Later that afternoon, back
with the Síraide.

Miach placed the Mountain's mugwort on the table. "For the moonwater," he said with his hands pointing to the north, where the Mothers' tent sat plumply. Their clan lived just beyond the circle of stone where the fire would burn that evening.

Long-Arm stopped at the doorway when Miach walked in. He had never enjoyed the confines of the long house, and today was no different. The meadow was his medicine, its waving plain his potion.

The room was filled with the delicate odor of many flowers. When a light westerly stirred about the garden, there came through the many small windows the subtle scent of Mountain Water or the more delicate color of children at play in the twisting dust.

Wind and laughter mixing.

Becoming the exhale.

Little feet giggling tornadoes 'round.

They were red.

Vast, welling guts of happy hearts.
I saw them smile.
I felt their smile.
I sent the devil of dust and leaves just for them,
To smile.

———————

From the far corner of the house in which the fire gently lay, a marvel of smoke rose up and out toward the great door of hewn oak and created strange clouds above the village.

A mantle of Robin and Raven feathers draped over the stone hearth, twisting in the wind and reflecting the fire's light across the hall. The feathers were arranged as ribbons of ribbed plumages upturned like brown and black blades. Swords they were—not of strength, but peace. An altar to Creator and also an altar to the liminal life. Fire and smoke. Creation and dreams.

The older brother's medicine was always more interested in the work of The Children of Cécht than the younger. Long-Arm did not particularly enjoy the enclosed space of the long house unless the winter's fire pulled him in—when stories became hearth-swollen and seared, slowly, over enflamed stars. When the ribbed feathers became alive.

It was too dark, too cramped under roof and beam, and he preferred the aroma of the moor's Art—incense clad in yellows and rising reds, wonderfully woven oranges fluttering by from the bright pink flowers of the meadow's milk, the piercing black hearts of the sun-wrapped susans, the dew walking upward when the hoof and heart splashed down.

That was his medicine, his Art.

That afternoon, Long-Arm walked around the corner of the

building, kicking a stone between the tents. He ambled like a moth in wont for flame, begging to burn, but slow. The Mountain lay heavy his mind. The stone circle, its mist. The bird, her words. A tasty pungency lingered in his heart, and he dawdled in the memory for some time. He watched the early afternoon Sun turn red and then a deep yellow as he swaddled the clouds.

Cumulus they were, I guess if I am to use your dull language.
Clouds that hold little water. Clouds that float just above an arm's reach. Clouds that call us upward.
Your boring wise men will call them cumulus, meaning heap or pile. Perhaps you call them that yourself.
Your tongue extending from the hearts of conquerors where the fluffy and loving collections of loosely held spring Mountain Water that play in bouncing whites and greys are rather called heaps.
Latin bastards.

But the clouds that day were not heaps like usual. This is the sign that The Mothers read. They were bluing into an ocean black, and the water was rising to meet them. The ocean was walking into the heavens.

———————

"I would rather you not," he said after a moment. The stone was melancholic and cracking. "I am already dusting into dirt," the stone continued after a brief pause.

The stone that Long-Arm busied himself with was round and carried a deep scar down his face from a tumble he took during a torrent long ago when he crashed into a jagged and storm-loosened

Mountain stone. When the season's flood pulled the moor up and the meadow down (for that is the point of floods), the two stones collided catastrophically, and this stone wore his wound with pride. As all river stones do. As this stone must. But his wound was now festering, and his end was near.

"I understand, my friend," Long-Arm responded squarely. "My apologies, I was not thinking."

"You were dreaming, and that is much better," the stone returned. "I enjoyed the ambling and was happy to dream with you, but now I am done. I am tired."

The boy squatted down and picked up the stone and rotated him in his hands like a leather ball. Long-Arm marveled at his smoothness, the gentle curvature, the grey grace. He walked to the Glei, a few paces to the south, and gently placed the stone in a once shallow but now growing bank where a network of larger stones, about a man in size, had created a babbling estuary.

Excited minnows fluttered in the water's silent circles, and the stone's color deepened as he descended from a rusting russet to black. Long-Arm lifted his fingers from the water and sat back.

"Be, my friend. And be still," Long-Arm said. "Tumble gently. Tumble slowly. But tumble into the valley moor, into your new beginning."

The stone did so.

———

Standing up, it happened that the boy felt the afternoon Sun cast a peculiar sheen over the small stream. An aroma of burnt Earth over acorns reflected through the air and animated his feet into ambling once again. The strange smell pulled him forward.

A biting bubbled into a rise from his toes as though he was standing on frozen ground, and he found himself carried over Mathgen's Mountain stone bridge and languidly approached, step over step, the outer canopy of the Star Oak. His eyes scanned for the source of the pungent smell. Nothing. He pivoted around, his toes tapping as they twisted, and his eyes fell back to the stream, now a distance behind him. Still, nothing. He could find no sign of the wild hearth. The aroma was surely close, but not sure.

After a while, weight shifting from his left to his right, he became uncomfortable and questioned if he smelled anything at all. Doubt crept in and he wondered why he cared so much, why the smell carried him so. He was busy playing with time, waiting for Miach, but the aroma was playing with him, sucking him in like inhaled breath.

"Hello," her voice said before he saw the subtle form plunking from the tree's upper branches.

A girl swung in the shadow of the canopy, colors shapeshifting from black to pink and then, ultimately, to a fine white. Her coral-colored buckskin pants now glittering in the dotted shade of the Star Oak's lower story. A small frame sitting gently on the tree's lowest limb.

"Your pants are wet," he said happily and happy now to find the source of the earthy smell.

"Kissed by the morning's mist," she replied.

"It's afternoon."

"Not on the Mountain," she said, smirking a fine white between her pursed red lips.

On her lap rested the flowered herbs that grow on stones, and her delicate fingers twisted and rotated their long stems around her thumb in spirals.

"They become flexible in time. You see?" she said without looking up but feeling his gaze upon her green jewelry. "At first, they are rigid and break when bent. But patience, I am told, makes even the rigid fold."

"I see," Long-Arm said. He was present and generally curious about the girl and her peculiar smell but distracted overall. He swung around the great trunk in a willful, petulant manner. He did not seem to care for the flowers and stems and her new jewelry, nor was he aware of the fact that she was on the Mountain that morning. He did, however, admire her ability to sit just so on the Oak's limb without even shifting her weight. It was unusual. She sat like a bird perched perfectly.

"What are you doing up there?" he asked incuriously.

"What are you doing down there?" she returned.

"I was helping that rock. You surely must've seen me at the stream," he said.

"I see many things. Did you want me to see?"

"I don't know," he said, embarrassed. He was not sure.

"What is your name?" she asked.

"Why do you want to know?" he returned quickly, turning his head just slightly.

"Why do you want to tell me?" she asked.

"Long-Arm," he responded without knowing why. "They call me Long-Arm. I am from the mane of Pryderi, of the yellow-black tents of the Horse clan."

"Yes, I know. I see you, often, running with her in the plains beyond," she responded, pointing her colorful and flower-wrapped fingers to the meadow that lay just outside the village.

"Then why did you ask my name?" he questioned.

"It is polite, no?"

"I guess," he said, admitting some ground.

"What were you before this?" she asked, now waving her decorated hands in circles. She twisted her head so that a strained lone eye looked down on him.

"She told me I was a wright—"

"She knows many things," the girl said, nodding effusively.

Long-Arm walked slowly to the other side of the Star Oak's canopy and pretended to play with the acorn at his feet. His fingers worked the cap off the nut, and he placed his thumb fully in the created center space. He pushed his calloused skin into the cap's crown. A strangely fine and familiar pain pulsed through him. After a brief smile that removed the cap from his thumb, he marveled at the white rim it left behind and the purpling mountain protruding in the middle. He placed his index finger on the purple mountain and pressed. The blood burst outward, and the white rim disappeared.

"That is what we call the harmony of transposition," she said, looking now over his shoulder.

The girl's voice startled the bending boy as it was closer than it should have been, given the distance he placed between them.

Looking up, he saw her unshod toes dangling only a few feet above his head. He smelled them before he saw them. They smelled like burnt acorns.

"The harmony of what?" he asked, this time with a tinge of burnt anger in his voice.

"I understand that you are familiar with harmony and resonance," she asserted.

"Yes. Are *you* familiar?" he asked, this morning's vision returning to him in a torrent of spring water.

"Is that your question?" she returned. Her voice lit his heart's flame like the strike of a match. The spring water sizzled into a boil between them. The Star Oak shivered.

"What does this have to do with acorns?" he asked.

"You live in this rimmed world, yes?" she asked.

"I guess," he said unconfidently.

"You guess?" she laughed. Her words cascading down in satire. "Where else do you think you live?"

"I—I don't know. I—I guess—I don't understand your questions," he said with blood now welling into his cheeks.

"Do you have to understand the meadow to walk it?" she asked, leaning forward. A smile alighting upon her pursed lips. "Is it knowledge that you want? Or the feeling of flowers and the colors of moist air wafting over you in galloping flight?" she leaned in even further. A smile broke laterally across her red lips. Something sinister and something also very kind.

"What is it you *really* want?" she asked.

The two figures were now so close that Long-Arm could smell her breath. An aroma of sweet carrion mixed kindly with savory grasses. It confused him. He could hear the beat of wings bouncing against the flap of hooves in her words, creating colors that he could taste and flavors that shivered as they sank deep into his spine.

"Stop it. Stop it!" He exclaimed, nearly shouting. He dropped both the acorn and its concave cap. He swung his arms freely, dismissing her questions, and then placed his hands in his pockets and started to walk away.

She was unmoved by his theatrics. "You held the rim of all future Oaks in your hand, and that future became a white rim in your own thumb, yes?"

The boy did not respond, but he found that his eyes were observing his thumb—the purple mountain, the white rim of the acorn's cap. His back was to the floating and tree-borne girl who asked too many questions.

"Your life was given to you?" she inserted the question into the stillness like a fire prod poking the winter's hearth.

"I guess," he said without turning around. His eyes were fixed on his thumb.

"And that acorn was given to you?"

"I guess," he said again. Her prodding now casting sparks that floated up into the canopy.

"And your name was given to you?"

"Yes," he said surely, feeling it snake between his lips.

"Names, like acorns and worlds, are not for those who wear them, or those who hold them, or even for those who live in them." She paused, feeling into the silence. After a moment, she continued, "They are for those who need them."

"And I am needed at the long house," he said as his feet stepped away from the tree's canopy. He was done and tired. Tiring fast.

"Goodbye...?" he asked, turning around only slightly and offering the question as the end.

"Rigu is fine for now," she said, swinging her legs freely from the limb.

"A strange name," he smirked.

"So is Long-Arm," she smiled. "Mine is a name you will soon need," she said.

"Hm," he coughed in response. Then, "As I said, goodbye."

"Names are beacons," she said just above a whisper, just to herself, just for her own journey, "beacons that bring the heavens down to walk with us," she paused and shook her arms like a Raven shakes its feathers. "They are like fallen stars and gods rising from the mounds."

Her eyes followed the boy across the village to the elusive and subtle smoke that floated out of the long house. It smelled like drowning dirt.

"Names are magnets of meaning," she whispered.

———————

Long-Arm did not hear her.

In fact, nothing of her last soliloquy made it far enough for him to hear. But his chest felt suddenly tight, though he couldn't understand why.

And so he walked on, tired and tiring fast of this conversation and conversation in general. He walked on, open-eyed and pondering.

He let the oak's crown and jewel fall from his hand upon the loose stone and dirt path. A field mouse fresh from the overgrown and drowning grasses growing astride the streambank shifted around it for a moment. Sniffing, it inspected the form. Searching, it scanned its rippled tan surface. But it moved on, empathetically, when a squirrel ambled in, snatching it for its larder.

The girl's words carried a sharp pain that panged through his body like a dull spear, poking as it punctured and leaving a rust to clot the wound. His eyes deepened into violet and then sparkled shyly, like amethyst.

"What does harmony and transposition have to do with names?" he thought to himself. "What was she doing in the tree?" he considered.

Behind him, Rigu, the shapeshifting girl who was now a Crow-Raven, spread her black wings and soared into the air. She passed over the tents like a shadow, and her shadow passed into the rising hills of the Mountain beyond, where the mist colors and covers even the strongest and straightest of stones.

The night's great fire was already being lit.

———

The People gathered at the long house just before sunset.

They walked from their tents of many colors and ambled together into the center of the village. A rainbow of light and a rainbow of kind.

This was The Mother's command: gather and walk to the fire together, entering as one people.

The village stepped through the wide stone threshold and yawning oak doors and stood still, their backs flickering against the hearth's low light. The hall was lit with the burning of swinging lamps that hung from the perfect oak beams. The once flower-filled tables now held many candles, tall and white, like tallow, burning brightly. A scent of juniper swaddled the thin air under a white veil.

"The Otherworld is close tonight," one said to another.

"Tonight," another responded.

"Yes, close," a third echoed back, their lips tasting the suspended perfume like wine.

At first, the aroma was pale-pink like mist over the morning meadow. Pale as the woven wings of the morning but silvering, soon, like the feathers of the pied wagtail in flight.

From their vantage in the long house, overlooking the village and the sprawling plain beyond, they saw, here and there over the growing stream and river that were together becoming a pond, reeds and willows sparkling their armory like stars, but lost in the deepening black-blue of the consuming waves. The water was growing and rising fast. The stars, the trees, losing. The Sun was setting. The dark pushing the light away. The trees pulling up the water like sponges, trying their best but suffocating, even the willows.

The People were now gathered and ready for the fire's altar. The Land, the seasons, the circle—their life depending upon the flame.

They ambled slowly from the long house to The Mothers' tents at the North of the village, where a great stone circle was already aflame, its grey plume floating up and calling them in.

Before they arrived, or really as they arrived, the Sun crested below the western horizon and exploded in one last orange-yellow-pink flare. To the south, The Mothers' fire had found the Mountain's *Snechtai*, The Snow rock, her white marble now coppice-clad in a crimson haze, a rosy miasma welling into the valley like red rainwater. These two lights called and carried The People on their way. These two lights reflected the colors of the world back on her people.

Teyrnon, the Ardent and the Stag, who had not been seen in the village since Long-Arm's pillar ceremony seven years ago, was standing astride the fire's flame. It splashed little shadows that flickered as they flew across his long nose. His antlers, now reaching toward the Mountain in dozens of pointed and spiraling tines, were clad in moss and hanging fabrics decorated by stones and colored in dyes of purple but dipped only halfway. He had the appearance of one who was long buried under the duff of the deep woods and had only recently emerged into the world.

The Mothers' fire typically tore the veil between their world and the Otherworld. It would pass their year into darkness. But it was not yet winter, and the veil was already torn. The Otherworld had walked among them and upon the ponding plain for days. It was already here, so the Mothers lit the fire for another reason: sacrifice.

————————

The fire lapped against itself and shot bright colors into the nearly starless night sky. It popped when stone met its maker and sizzled when the fuel's heartwood released its Waters. Ageless living wells bursting outward when the fire found its way in.

"I am the god who gives you fire," the flame echoed as The People entered the circle.

"And we are The People who receive it," they echoed in harmony, removing their shoes. This was holy ground.

Miach led the village into the fire's circle. This was his father's role at fires past. But life was different now that Cían was gone (dead?), everyone understood, and Miach accepted his role willingly.

He carried the morning's mugwort in the Caldron, and his fingers paled into a white-pink under its thin rim. The mugwort had been sufficiently worked by the herbalists, and she was ready for the Water. The Moon steadily rose into her fullness, and the second light enflamed the rising night with a strange gravity.

The dew arose from the soil below their feet. Water sprinkled upward. The river Cailleach rushed beyond the circle. The white second light of the Moon sparkled under her now foaming and surging surface, and the white willows furrowed their bark an inch more. The fig-mulberries dropped their five-lobed leaves in an orange-red rain, and the oaks were silent—for it was they who talked in clouds.

It was they who hushed the Moon.

They who called to The Mothers.

It was they who knew what was coming.

"Our poet, Cairbre, is no longer with us," one Mother said after a long pause that lasted many hours.

The night was now fully into her darkness, and the Moon was cresting westward but silent. The fire was strong and bright.

"His body," the Mother continued, "washed up the Cailleach this morning. His tongue ripped out and his eyes gouged with hot irons. His body was grey and blueing into black."

The People were silent, listening. The Plant clan, Cairbre's clan, wailed a twisting song just above a windy whisper and danced a pale green against the rising flame in sorrow. One flower, who was standing at the fire's feet, extended upward, uncurling her infinite colors, and sang,

> O lithe as a willow-weave!
> O sea passing the bounder!
> O tails creeping the river mares!
> O Earth now less the rounder!
> O winter-time our catalyst!
> O colors laconic and dull again after!
> O roots without rot, long live the sleeping satirist!

Everyone, as one, then wept.

The fire steamed a pulsing orange. It purled into a fine blue. The Children of Cécht then stepped forward with their rowan tree-banded braids of medicine. They looked at The Mothers, and The Mothers nodded back. Sight carried through flame.

The Children then handed the Robin clan the rue for listening, the Plant clan the sage for swelling, the Horse clan the vervain for spirit, and the Stag clan the wort for dreaming. The Crow-Raven clan, The Mothers, sat silently by as each clan dropped the woven-earth bundles into the fire.

The Horse dropped the bundles of vervain first, and the spirit ascended in crackling sparks. A peculiar and durable weightlessness settled, and the hearts of The People floated into the air like loosed helium.

The Stag then tossed the wort into the flame, and a black dreamsmoke descended down like a backdraft in the night's open chimney. A thick gravity cemented toe into clay, and The People fell into hypnosis, images becoming real as their heart-minds walked through flame and dancing shadows.

After some time, the Robin placed the rue into the fire, and it exploded with popping rocks. This was the climax, and it was a special moment to behold. The ears and eyes of The People's hearts opened, and they listened to the soundless deep of the night sky, the Moon's drifting cry, of the heavens reaching out to them in sparkling warp threads. They danced and twirled like leaves set free in a strong wind, and they sang and lay together, seeking pleasure for the pain that was easily procured and common.

The white wood of the wise oak that burned in the fire turned into a fine caramel when the blue and orange flame found the rue and lapped at length against the sky. It lapped the night long, and it lapped as The People's feet struck and pounded and slapped Earth down. The mycelia below pulsed like energy through wires but better, but actual—intimate. This caused the trees around to shiver and shake and the flowers and soused summer grasses to wave as it pulsed up their vascular veins. Life danced with her people. The wise oak flamed under splashing love and burnt herbs.

At length, the caramel wood deepened into black when the fire let herself in—the flame and wood fibers becoming one. The settled heat, the subtle pulse of Oneness.

Nearing the dawn, the Plants placed the bundles of sage into the now dawdling flame and all receded into a calm stillness—all fell into a protracted silence. Life lingering on the liminal. Silent and patient. Loving and dreaming of love. They lay for some time.

The People and The Mothers and the fire then woke and watched as the Sun crested the eastern hills. They looked as he broke upon the new day like shattered glass. Energy bursting as light, sound falling as silence.

The Cailleach's Waters settled in the belly of the Caldron, the white willows stopped their waving, and the dew dropped into her place.

The morning, fresh and now calm and calming, was here.

The light, holy and now clean and cleansing, had won.

At this, the Old Mother stepped forward and presented herself to the fire, its flame, and its people. Her arms held herbs and loose leaves. Her lithe lips, one side curling and showing the white underneath. Her bent and bloated back, a core searching for metaphor. Her infinite age working outward in gnarled fingers and flaked yellow nails.

She was age itself. Every move, everything she did, was strobed by the light that dappled and writhed about her. The morning, the dawdling flame, the Old Mother, the Land herself. She, the leader of The People. The Ancient One.

The red tectonics that shift and rise and rip under our feet could be seen, often, rippling through a purple translucence of veins that bulged to a point in her forehead. She was the ageless immersion and boundless engagement of the immortal language of stars and of the Moon and their gravity sprinkling upwards.

Life, it seemed, waited patiently upon the silvery spine of her words. So also did The People.

"The Moon is not right," she said, standing straight and focused on the Caldron at her feet.

The clay basin held the light of the Moon under its rim, and the mugwort drifted down into its depths. A camphoric smell like old mothballs admixed with the bitterness rising from the water. A light shone from the Caldron and lit the Old Mother's chin from underneath.

"The Moon," she continued, "never fell to become new. Full to full, she has lived in the unnatural light of life for too long." The Old Mother ushered a tear obscuring her view. "Darkness is coming, but it is not hers," she said, looking up and into the eyes of those around her.

A heart scything through them, an ageless eye piercing theirs.

Everyone was silent.

Breathing but barely.

Then, a noise filled the air.

A horrible, curdling noise like twisted chords, filled with pain and aged fears and also a silvery-white beauty like long years. It was beautiful and horrible. It was awful and awesome. It was light and dark and it emanated from the animated tips of the Old Mother's silvery hairs. The hairs curled and twisted as though they were being burned alive. They screamed a shrill in a pitch nearly inaudible, but one that everyone, everything, could feel deeply.

After a long pause, she continued, "Long have the Oceaners ruled over this Land. Their unnatural tendril fetid and thrusting into the fabric of our life. Our knives forever without grease, hospitality and honor lacking at every meal. The Oceaners stole our music, but now they come to take what is left. There is water everywhere but nothing to drink. There is milk in empty pales.

"The *Máithrín* is not in her season, and the Cailleach's Waters bubble and foam but not over rock and stone. We are the deep wells of Water, the music that lives, that resonates with the pillars in the plain. It is this that gives life her beauty, and it is this that gives the living their life—the Water goes in, and our blood comes out.

"But," she continued without inhaling, "the Water is rising. The Land screams like hairs combed in the wrong direction." She spoke with a deep and surprising emotion. Emotion like a life ending. Emotion like fire falling.

"Swallow, swallow, little swallow, what a mess they have made," she said after a gravid pause, her words choked under tears.

At this, she fell back and lay in the dirt.

"They are coming," she said, staring at the sky.

The dew was linen now, and heavy.

Bacharigu then walked forward. She had been silent until this point. She was patience waiting for her moment. The girl passed beyond the Old Mother, her coral-colored buckskin pants reflecting the rising morning light against the Ardent's tines. The dawn now fully alighting his face.

She nodded at him. He nodded back. The ageless scars of Mountain stone shone a fine white against his skull.

She smiled at him. He smiled back. A tear welled and fell. A wing sprouted behind her left shoulder. Another tear, another silent moment. Then, another wing.

She flew away to prepare.

They were not coming.

They were already here.

Later that morning,
in the village.

It was not long until The People heard the drumming of the Oceaners. The dew was deep into its work when the *boom* and *doom* echoed over the valley, and Pryderi nickered into a roar as her feet galloped to the long house to warn the village.

She was grazing at the valley's edge where the hill's rise falls upward at the feet of the Mountain, and the grasses struggle to grow. It was the last reserve of higher ground, and the grasses tried their best to grow. The landscape below was now a shallow pond, a moor becoming marine, the ocean letting itself in. The rocky uplands were the last reprieve, a lone island of hope. Not much, but some.

The mare often ambled this far from the village for the peace and quietude its stillness supplied. There were herbs here that flowered into phallic medicines. They have no name, but she knew them as smooth-headed spear caps. This morning, however, after the fire ceremony, she sought a last meal.

A deep *doom* rumbled over the hills and rising Waters and startled her into motion, thin blades of grass still adrift in her lips. Running back to the village to warn The People of the rolling Oceaner wave, the wind fully alighting her mane like a great swell, she thought she saw a white Horse astride her shadowless side. From the corner of her eye it seemed so. But she ran on. And when she turned to face the galloping color, it disappeared. But she could feel its secondary gallop, she could feel its presence next to her, its cresting harmony. The late morning alighted from the heights and sparkled symbols all around the valley, but every time she turned her muzzle to look, to attempt to see, the white disappeared into shadow.

She was alone but not lonely. The white Horse was there but also not there. A peculiar warmth tickled her spine, and a strong kindness seemed to cover her.

Pryderi crossed the great meadow in dashing splashes that threw the shallow water hither, and a foam-washed wake ran behind her. This was not the plain of her memory, but its internal nature was known to her—she knew where its topography rose and fell, where it twisted and careened into shallow gullies or rose into miniature Mountains. Her feet, unshod, struck the soil with care and intimacy as she barreled over the Waters to the village.

———————

The meadow glistened in front of her.

The plain was painted in what looked like blue-tinged spruce lost in adolescence. Green and black and brown tipped by enflamed white and burning red striped berries. Each spruce waved the late morning awake, curling and uncurling in the cascading light and the Horse's strong wind.

These woody and winter-loving plants were all that lived in the thalweg of the plain. Their roots were deep and capable of extending beyond the filling pond Waters.

They were accustomed to the climate's change.

And they prepared for the long winter.

———————

Pryderi's feet slid to a halt on the stone mantle of the long house.

"They are here," she said to the herbalists.

The Children groaned in reply but were steady in their work.

She then ran to the Glei and over Mathgen's bridge of Mountain stone and approached the Star Oak solemnly.

"They are here," she said to the Oak.

The Oak shivered, but no acorns were let fall.

She then ran to The Mothers' tent, the circle of blackened logs and white ash shaking as she passed, but the Old Mother was dreaming and a thin voice, an echo of the river's reeds, told her onward.

"Send you the river," she whispered.

The mare went on.

She then fell into the oak and willow glen growing astride the great river Cailleach.

"They are here," she said to the river.

"Yes, I know," the river returned, bubbling a foam that twisted and twirled into a little hurricane of white-brown life, of water dusting into dirt.

"What are we to do?" Pryderi nickered, her eyes circling with the river's foam.

"Be at peace," the river Cailleach said.

"You have given me many children. You have been kind to let me bring up your young," Pryderi said. "But the Oceaners have already taken two-thirds of the mare's milk, and now they are coming to take the mare herself." Her fearlessness faltered into courage and then, soon, dwindled into fear itself.

"Fear is faith in the wrong direction," the river Cailleach said. "You asked me what to do. I told you, be at peace."

"They are here to take your mare and the river's daughters, your children," Pryderi returned, this time in a panic, stomping a hoof as she paced the riverbank. The solid Earth rumbled and shook.

"They can take the mares if they like. They will take my children if they will. But they can never have them. They can never have you. Be at peace," the river Cailleach said. "I have sent one to help," the river Cailleach continued. "She is already deep into her work. You may know her as a white Horse that runs with you, or as the Raven whose shadow stands always before you in the meadow, or as the girl in coral."

"I have seen a girl with Long-Arm," Pryderi returned. "Is this who you mean? She wears buckskin pants."

"Yes. I have sent one to help," the river Cailleach said.

"I saw her talking with him under the Star Oak, and he told me, after his return from the Mountain, that a scald-crow found him there as well," returned the mare, the story building now fully into itself for the first time in her heart.

"Be at peace," the river Cailleach said, "but do not let passivity destroy you. Flow, run, gallop in a torrent. When the grey storm rises, its winds of biting and cutting steel shape stone and their soil into a soliloquy, a wrecking semblance. But then it ends. Simple. And calm. Smiling. Rise and smash what you must. Rise and cleanse this Land in a great torrent. Let steel bite and cut what it must. But then, find peace."

At this, Pryderi trotted back through the glen, slowly. She stepped through the village of innumerable tents of many colors spread like autumn leaves. She slowed to a walk as she crossed over the Glei's stone bridge.

"Thank you," one of the stones whispered as she passed.

"For what?" she returned without stopping.

"For bringing us the boy."

———————

The Oceaners' train slithered through the valley and over the shallow Waters, a water snake skating just above the glass and sad surface. A water snake at home in its environment, coiled and ready to strike.

The bald heights that towered above were adorned by the crowning *Máithrín*, and life looked down sadly upon their ranks, their unnatural form. The Oceaners' drummers pounded rhythmically upon ocean stones, and a deep *boom* and *doom* carried the army in step.

Balor, their god-king, was called The Piercing Eye, for his eyes had been poisoned by the dark arts long ago, and they also poisoned whatever they beheld. When his lids were open, his eyes transformed trees into javelin shafts, forests into pulp that rowan red fires would employ to melt steel, and the love of the Land would curdle and curl like spoiled milk. When his lids were let fall, his eyes destroyed himself.

"A muscle that opens and closes the crab's claw," the Old Mother whispered to herself. She was sitting in front of her tent that over looked the long valley.

A subtle breeze lifted the plain and was bitter with the smell of bruised tannins. The invading army slithered near.

Colors rusting.

Colors rotting.

The Oceaners came over the Land as a mounting wave that stalked the plain with dark blue raiment and foam-crusted mail glimmering a gloom of silver.

The Old Mother watched as murders of crows and their attending mockingbirds flitted away in units of two and three as the deep drums reverberated and lapped over the plain like a wave over a reef. She watched as the curlews specked from the swelling bogs. They flashed a shadow over mottled stone before dipping beyond the horizon. They were leaving—leaving the plain and her pillars to their fates.

In the Old Mother's hands was a small sharp knife. It was tipped with her palm's blood that trickled into the clay. A final offering. Around her scrambled the busy feet of The People, and a subtle mist floated about the knees of the village. Everything was the color of dust.

The People saw torches scattering below like horrid flowers. Countless metal points reflecting the Sun like pallid pools. The Waters below uttering a response. A steam rose in front of them, and a solid black muck fell behind.

"They are burning as they go!" one of The People cried in terror.

"Would that day be glad that we may ride down to meet them and fall upon their ranks like a tumbling stone!" another fumed.

"Great grief settles upon this Land," the first returned, "and great sadness falls upon her Síraide."

Their minds flared, found purchase, and fell into their work. The smiths busied by sharpening iron. The herbalists prepared the Caldron. The wrights crafted wheels for war carts and wooden shields as well. But the Old Mother, like a rotten log in a cut forest, sat still. Her eyes watched the snake slither through the plain. Her hands leaked a steady drip of life back into the soil, a reverse pillar. Her heart pounded slightly above a susurration. Confusion tumbled around her. A virulent chaos swung the lit of lamps above her head. But she was still. Her blood trickled silently into Earth.

"Today, a day of days," she murmured with her eyes closed and her heart open. Her palm pulsed. "Today, blood of my blood. Today, Earth of my Earth. We will fall."

Her voice strained and fell as it splashed into the shapeless and moist clay. "But how will we rise?"

————

Breoch, Balor's son who was born of the sea-borne tryst between the ocean and the Land, had waited for this moment in the moors beyond the Rim of the world.

He was raised by the Land but kept one foot in the water and nestled, finely, under its great peat. In this way, he grew two years for his every one. One foot on the Land and one foot in the water, but only one heart set on The People's destruction. On his finger, he wore the thumb-ring given to him by his mother and that which Balor gave to her.

This morning, as the Oceaners journeyed across the drowning plain, Breoch joined his father.

"Welcome, father," the boy said.

"Watch and learn," Balor returned without looking.

"I will do more," the boy said.

"You will do enough," Balor retorted.

The boy's ring sparkled under the passing Sun.

"She said it was yours," the boy said, feeling his father's heart beat within the ring.

"It is yours now. Watch and learn."

And so he did.

————

The dew's linen was pulled when their train reached the long house. Balor stepped forward regally, and the drums halted as his hands lifted. A strange silence fluttered across the village. A pallid and rotting aroma of carrion cladding the air. A smell immoderately salted.

Late autumn leaves crashed without sound and circled a burnt yellow in the grey mist at their feet. But no valley breath, no soft breeze lifted the tree's litter. They and their People waved and waned in a silent sadness.

It was not a silence well known in the village. It was not created from hushed breath but from no breath at all. A vacuum of life and not a halt in its motion. The village shifted its weight, together, as though to kickstart Earth's rotation. But everything was still. Everyone was silent, like lungs held under ocean water.

"King, welcome to the plain," Teyrnon said, breaking the silence as he walked forward.

"*Our* king!" one Oceaner captain returned, dropping his spear toward the head of the Stag.

"Our king, welcome," Pryderi said, stepping between the spear and the Ardent. The river Cailleach's words worked deep within her. "Our king, how can we serve you?" she inquired.

"What cause is such a bad aspect?" Balor questioned with a gurgle. "Is my rule and Breoch, my son, not enough?" he asked, presenting a shell-encrusted and salt-softened wooden box.

The People shifted again, curious in fear. The Mountain's heart worked through them, but quietly. They were a singular body energized by the memory of music, but a sadness and horror played through them, individually.

At this, Balor opened the box and grabbed the knotted blonde threads that lay inside the wooden chest and lifted the bloody mass for all to see. Cían, Miach's father, the weaver of power and an Ambassador, dripping bloody tears from serrated and sawed muscle and bone, dangled from the king's hand. The head's eyes were crossed and his tongue, limp and lurid, hung like autumn apples.

The People, especially the Plants, wailed and released a mourning shriek. Some collapsed in pain, wilting, and others stepped forward in anger.

Balor's attendants lowered their spears further and stayed any rebellion.

"It is not about sufficiency," Pryderi said, unable to look away from the loosed head of her friend.

"No?" The king's swollen tongue played with the syllable.

"No," Pryderi said. "To make our plain a pond, to litter our river's Waters with ocean salt, to empty our pales once filled, is to take from us that which is us. You take forcibly what we would have given to you willingly, and in doing so, you take everything and transform us into nothing."

"I think Cairbre and this Cían," one of the king's attendants mocked with hands flailing at the dripping head, "were highly flattered."

"Yes—well, flattened perhaps!" another attendant teased back, and the whole army slithered into satire.

Pryderi's anger mounted, and a fine red fell into shadow upon her eyes. "Be at peace," again the river Cailleach's voice rose above the miasma of mocking pain. But blood rushed into her hooves, flirting with founder, and her body tensed without release.

She caught the eye of the Old Mother just to her right, who wore an opaque but calm façade. So she turned to the left, to Teyrnon, who wore the omen of stone. Ageless patience.

"Cairbre's body floated like a plant loosed in the current," Balor said, his voice breaking the silence. "It hung in the shallows like lost kelp, his eyes picked clean by ocean waves, and his legs, sallow and swollen, were like sand under the leaving tide. Our tide. We cut out his tongue and feasted well."

"And Cían? Why?" Miach stumbled forward painfully, a tear welling but never cresting its duct. His hands, both of them, whitening into fists.

"Ah yes!" the king returned slyly, his tongue again playing between his teeth. He repositioned his curved scabbard hanging from his belt. His fingers rolled over the blue gems of ocean water encrusted upon

the sword's hilt, its reddening rust crackling. At this and after a sharp
pause, he said,

> Far under the ocean snow
> The fire it roared, a bellow boiling.
> Your father, he fell, away and below.
> A waning wail in flame he spread,
> Into the cavern that holds the dead.

The Oceaners fell into deep laughter. Borne over the dark it erupted
as the sound of harsh cantillation and collided with the dust and
formed many sharp and drifting particles that punched as they fell. It
was noon, but the Sun fell fast.

Balor's eye was now open, held so by his attendants. The sky became
utterly dark and covered the Land in black scudding clouds. A silver
stillness of the heavy air told of a storm, but no thrashing would come.
The Underworld was at work.

Then, shakes. A swift dash of blinding light flashed from a chasm
that cleft between them. Earth split as the ground gave way. A great
tremble thrashed at their feet like a dying fish, but worse. It quivered
into a quake. The wound, the awful suppurating rip, oozed clay from
once solid rock. The Land bled. The Land shook and rumbled. The
Old Mother closed her eyes.

Branched lightning like overturned roots climbed upward and
scurried out of the dark blue cavern.

Light searching for something.

Never finding.

Repeating.

The lightning slithered across the boiling plain and charred The
People's pillars into a fine black soot. Another blinding light dashed
an echo from the assailing deep, and, this time faster than the first, it
collided with the Mountain like a spear. It summited like rising rain,

but searing and hot. It then fell upon the bald heights and then, next, upon the *Máithrín*. A dark tide thundered back across the valley. A roar rumbled its anger. But no rain lashed down.

Balor then closed his eye and the branched light flickered and fell away and the chasm closed as instantly as it came. The clouds peeled and parted, and all fell as it was. A painful silence floated over the Land, but peace did not return—not yet.

The Old Mother liberated a tear and let it drop into the chasm before it closed.

"Become peace," she thought. "Become," she dreamed.

————

"We have not come for peace," one of Balor's attendants read from a curled scroll made from dried kelp.

Its letters and symbols were scratched by sharp coral that was ripped from their beds and hewn for the purpose.

Pryderi whickered under her breath, and a light plume of smoke flitted from her nostril.

The Oceaner continued reading without noticing the smoke. "We have come to exact a tax, not upon your living, but upon your life." Looking up, he said, "You are shaped by the Land for her purposes. Today, you will shape the Land for ours."

"Give us the Ardent, the maker of altar and stone, the Stag of the Mountain's soul," another Oceaner demanded. "Today, we will sacrifice to cleanse this Land of its metamorphosis. Today, we will end your tomorrows."

There were no clouds in the sky overhead. The Sun was lacking, missing, and dark. A heaviness descended like rain but dry and shifted like sandy spears thrust over the desert's dunes. All light was blurred. Then, behind the dim, in the east, rose slowly up the sky a deeper darkness. A great storm was curdling, but its shadow was already here, fully.

Death was at the door, but it was an undying death.

Teyrnon dropped back behind Pryderi and his gaze caught Miach's. The boy's deep green eyes welling fully into tears.

"Death of death, a sinking pallid death," the boy thought. Miach's surroundings often inhabited him, colors possessed him, worked through him until he was moved by all of the forces at once.

Under the rising darkness, a strange energy pulsed up and through his feet and flowed steadily until it raptured him in dream. The Harp's ancient and lost music swelled in him. Her words foamed into a fine clay and then found their place as a molten iron in his heart.

This is the most ancient color that all speak. A language that all understand and are capable of carrying: it is love.

It is older than the Mountains and older even than the bubbling brooks that babble from the deep wells of Water. More ancient than the great trees that created all and in all were created.

To capture it, to become clothed by it, two eyes must be met.

It is color that gives our dreams meaning.

It is love that gives harmony its resonance.

"It is love," Miach said to himself, below a whisper, a tear falling into its place. His eyes fell upon Teyrnon. "Death, my death, it is love," his eyes said when they fell on the Ardent.

It was at this that he heard, like you hear me now, certain words descend from the trees around him. The Star Oak shivered in a windless draught and a wild calmness ushered the boy deeper, deeper into dreaming.

"From the vastness of the heavens to the unformed floors under the infinite duff of the deep oak woods—" the words sprinkled around him like spring loosened daffodil flowers or like the white willow down that float a sparkling spring of silvery snow, "—humanity scintillates an intimacy assembled from a quick smile, a turning glance," the voice said, and he recognized it now.

The mugwort's simple words, his mother's words, echoed against the chaos around him. He remembered her smile, that great arching light, that which animated and alit her life when she spoke about his kind.

Her words in him now flowed like water through sand.

And then suddenly, but not harshly, they stopped—the dream and the mugwort's words. He stammered back, overcome with surprise like one who wakes too quickly from slumber. He looked urgently around the chaos of the coming tide and found Teyrnon once again.

Balor's attendants were stepping to the Stag. The Stag was stepping to them. They were close now.

"Death, my death," Miach's heart screamed the words of the mugwort back to the world. At this, the Mountain spat a strong and sure wind, and a small ball of blue flame burst and then fizzed on the ground where the spit landed.

"The most ancient color is that which all speak," her words again. "To become clothed by it, two eyes must be met."

Miach's gaze fell from the Mountain and back onto that which lay upon him—the pain, the chaos, the coming end. His eyes then found Teyrnon, and a peculiar energy met the heavens home.

The Stag nodded, understanding.

Miach nodded back, a smile's small split finding the tip of his lips.

At this, the son of mugwort lunged forward, his veined blades glittering and then closing the space between. A calligraphy of cries fell where Earth had cleft only moments before, and a deluge of thin watery blood splattered in loose mottled puddles as his sharp blade ripped the ecstasy from the Oceaners' inhuman faces.

With great speed and between blinks, Miach replaced their snide smiles with leatherless and smeared purpling muscles and cheekbones that burned like pyres. Blood black as misery splattered across his breast when his blade found their inner and loveless cores. His robes became stained by loosed bowls. A putrid green found a stagnant yellow as it rose from the exposed offal, the leaking stomachs. It smelled like rotting fish.

He stepped over liberated leg and limb and strode to Breoch—the boy-king granitic in name only. But a foreign blade hissed above his head. With the agility of a god, for a god he was, he grabbed the face of the iron instrument and studied it.

Blink.

It was warm, as though it had been heated by the skin of another.

Blink.

It was blue, as though it was crafted and honed and shaped in the tears of falling forests and stripping ocean waves.

Blink.

It was curved and serrated, flecks of flesh still hanging like jerky from its dull rivulets.

Miach threw the sword of his enemy to the side and worked toward the boy-king. A rush of attendants seized the scurry like storm wind in the branches of the maple tree and fell before him. A chaos of parleys ensued. But the boy was quickly victorious.

The lone leech then leapt like a leaf loosed in a storm and dropped a raining blow that severed the left arm from the boy-king at his shoulder. The thumb-ring tumbled into the dirt and dissolved like ice under salt or lust under love. The Land then rose like a snake and swallowed what was left, taking back what had been taken from her.

At this, Balor fell upon Miach and lowered his spear a hair's breadth from his heart. Light like a lightning snap in the otherwise lightless night stalled the chaos instantly, and the impromptu battle settled into silence.

Breoch wailed inaudibly, his pain too great, as Balor's lone surviving attendant lifted his eye's lid.

"What are you?" he inquired, looking for the boy.

"I am Miach, the son of mugwort and the great medicine man. Cían is my father," the boy replied, wiping the blood from his lips, the coagulated red-purple miasma smearing like snot.

"*Was* your father," Balor returned.

"The evil do not win—not finally," the boy replied. "No matter how loud they are."

"Your father sank like a fallen log," Balor said, smiling, mocking.

"What slave fails to render his master's decay?" the boy replied, smiling back.

Then, with a tear animating into a leafy liquid spear, the boy closed his eyes and dreamed. He closed his eyes and saw Teyrnon. He closed his eyes.

"That is love," he said with emotion staying the clarity of each syllable, the words, especially the last, losing their intonation as they fell. He spoke simply and without looking.

Energy emanating from his sensorium triggered a pulse through his neck and shoulders that landed, finally and ultimately, in his fingers. His veins seemed to burst when the energy pushed through them, leaving little bumps, like the feather-plucked skin of the goose, in its wake. The evolutionary defense to make oneself look bigger, more dangerous perhaps. Or the ecstasy of pleasure, remembered or otherwise, of hairs standing straight in love or in being loved. Either way, Miach smiled as his fingers shook slightly and curled under the welcome and familiar emotion.

Everyone, now standing in the circle, The People and the Oceaners alike, even the one-armed boy-king, looked at Miach and were silent. The wind stilled and the dust, once drifting, stayed for the moment. A swallow flicked by and halted its late autumn migration on the lowest branch of the Star Oak. It paused to pay its respect to the medicine man. It sung its cackling click and then flew toward the south.

Miach then looked at Balor, his gentle eyes shining what little light was left. He nodded, giving permission.

Balor then thrust his spear through the heart of the boy, and Miach curled forward. He fell into his last inhale. A plant withering under the swelling storm. A leaf wilting and bending closed. A hushed silence collapsed like silvery linens of dew. No one, not even the spear, dared to move.

A tear fell from Miach's eye as his body stood still and then more tears followed. He looked straight into Balor, peering into his poisoned pupil. Balor looked back. Miach looked down at the red slowly veining over the sharpened steel that was protruding from his chest. Balor looked down at his own hands holding the rough wooden shaft. They looked up. Together. They saw each other and held each other's gaze for the moment. Just the moment.

"Love clothed when two eyes be met," whispered the wind. Then the boy, before entering death's door, closed his eyes and incanted,

O! White the willow down.
O! The spring flower.
Wind over the Waters, the dew becoming a shower.
Dingle, dingle, dangle
The moss its grasp entangles.
The stone, its age, our life and spangle.
The lapping shores our lapis,
The wind-swept sea our limit.
Dingle, dingle, dangle
The music, the dancing pillars, a fine feather.
But I have heft the king from his throne,
Of Sun and Moon and rising weather,
O! White the willow down.
O! The spring flower.
Without his arm the boy-king is without his power.

Hearing this and fearing that he may succumb to this satire, Balor twisted the spear and then removed the point from the boy's heart with a simple pluck, and Miach fell face-first into the dust.

He lay motionless.

He lay.

At peace.

The Oceaners dissipated like a low tide.

The Síraide gathered around Miach's body, a low hum animating their steps. Teyrnon was the first to get to him and rolled him over.

The boy was smiling.

"No one moves alone," the Stag said, now crying intensely and gently playing with the boy's hand with his own. He embraced Miach's palm with his lips, wet with tears and wet with a teary mucus. He kissed one hand and then kissed the other. "Thank you, my friend."

The severed and dying Oceaners bloated lonelily under the afternoon Sun like stale pufferfish. Their bodies distended and ready to burst.

"Today was enough," Balor whispered to Breoch as they walked away, "but we are far from done. Our religion is a culture, and like all invading cultures, it is very good at destroying what lived before it."

"What or who?" Breoch replied, holding the nub of his arm to stall the blood, his face wincing in the pain that was ebbing to an end.

"Both—we will destroy both."

———

It has been a while since I checked in. I am sorry for that. The story is becoming something to tell and I have been lost in my work.

I want to talk to you, only briefly, about Miach's song. His words etch the dimensions of this Land.

I want to talk to you about Miach of the Plant clan, the medicine man that you will call a sorcerer. His children you will burn in the streets. Their language you will force from them. You will tell them to cut their hair and speak the Oceaner speak, that language that dominates the world. This language.

I believe this is because you have never understood him or taken the time to try. You never looked into his eyes. Because, if you did, then you would not be as you are.

And so I want to talk to you about the boy whose smile is covered in dust. I want to tell you this story so that, while you will never be able to look into his eyes, not fully, we can attempt something else.

Maybe, just maybe, there is still time.

Utopia's story, the pious servitude to the idea that progress solves problems, is well peddled by the dominant few—the guiled grifters of civilization. The Oceaners: the saints and the salesmen. You are simultaneously a people and the product of a people suffering not from a crisis but a worldview—a dominating worldview of bigots.

You don't believe me?

That is expected. I am only a Crow-Raven.

It is written in exposed clay and colored by black rainbows of the millions of years consumed in moments, and the handwriting looks eerily like your own.

Your ancestors burn around you, effigies of old stories forced into old courtyards that smell of witchy offal and burnt hair and bones. You may not like the smell, for it suffocates your mammalian lungs, but you accept its potpourri as the byproduct of your life and the machines that are strangely the source of your power and the source of your pain.

There is no room for heretics who talk to land and not to landowners, those uncommitted to incumbency, those untethered to tenure. If you need a new story, then you need the heretic's old story. But that story is long burned in your waste bins. That story is not useful. But it is that story that I am trying to tell you...trying. Your waste bins are deep.

But dingle, dingle, dangle echoes against your plastic clothed and air-tight abodes alongside city walls and dusk-covered concrete aisles that usher the working dead home, where already plated microwave dinners unaided by anything that looks like love provide the fuel for the fire to burn just one more day. Just one more day. You burn.

That humans create is true.

That humans create well is the eternal question.

I am telling you this story so that you open your eyes. But not so that you can see. No, that will come.

I am telling this story so that you can look at me.

One Lunar Cycle later.

Around the time of the new Moon, he came upon the early dusk of evening, and drawing near, he saw the light of lamps dancing in the windows. The wind-swept marsh reeds that grew far below kept a wide berth. A shadow dappled the Ash outside of the long house, the reliquary of all that was left.

Long-Arm was adrift. He was floating under the familiarity of dusk, the soon hiemal sky. Her deep grey paling into a pink and serous rose, if only momentarily. The mundane, the beautiful lapped and lacquered by a strange ugliness.

That is why he was floating. His anchor had been cut.

Life co-existed with the terror that walked their streets. Life trying to smile but with lips too encumbered by lies to do any good. This was the life of the village after Miach's death. It was denuded and threatening collapse.

The Oceaners reduced The People's tents, or *lavvu,* to ash upon the first night of their arrival in a great and gyrating pyre. They danced around the flame and drank as the leather burned. A sulfurous bouquet echoed when the heat found the cysteine locked within the hides' hair, and a great wheezing whine burst from the lapping and dancing flames.

Like life burning alive.

Like life burning.

Burn.

Even Balor, his eye closed as he sat astride the fire in a makeshift throne of staves and sheep skins, danced with his fingers. He played in a rhythm pinky first that rolled slowly, finger by finger, to his thumb. The linear melody splashed down and splashed again. Both hands in unison, working together to tap, tap, tap the fire into a rolling and twisting might.

His hair was tonsured, cut after Miach's death, and the flame shone a strange light against the bald skin atop the rim of hair. A forced crown of the forced king. A forced crown seeking religious solidarity for their empire's sake. There would be no room for heretics, only heralds and priests and pilgrims.

Breoch, in his first and last order as the boy-king, for his arm was festering now, forced the village to live within the great hall or to succumb to the open nights of autumn. He burned their tents into ash—unnatural, the smell of decay reached out without rot.

The People mourned as they moved into the long house.

Long-Arm's anchor was Miach.

As he ambled aimlessly about the tentless village and under the ashen and wintering sky, thoughts of his brother floated loosely in front of him. He fondly remembered the days when Miach walked with him. He remembered the moments they shared and the moments when the medicine man would leave him at the door of the long house as he strode into the darkness of the hall to work the medicines.

Herbalists, always at work but never working. Herbs, always working but never at work. But Miach, both herb and herbalist, was dead.

Long-Arm remembered how his brother talked about the smells and the signs of the coming seasons. Miach's endless search for flowers and roots and mushrooms to hold in the apothecary, to hold for the village for when they would be needed—the herbs and their herbalist.

"Some loose stones under galloping thunder. Others seek the life caked under fields and upon the flaxenhaired fairylands," he thought to himself, his brother's words alive in the air inside of his chest. "But all," Miach's memory returned in a gentle whisper, "are the medicine."

Long-Arm's dusk dawdling landed him in front of the long house. He paused in the doorway. Breath held and swelling. The pain of Miach's death becoming real and growing legs the closer he neared. He stood under the great oak passageway pensively. Then, exhaling, he walked in slowly, letting his eyes adjust to the dim light.

Once inside, he saw that its rafters were sullen in mourning and creaked, strangely, like those settling, finally, after being shaped and placed. There was a sad newness to the hall, and new medicine wafted from the stone below the great hearth.

There was no fire in the place. A black hearth below black bird feathers that shimmered only slightly in the darkness. The medicine's smell was peculiar but inviting, strong but kind.

The night following Miach's passing, The People buried the boy under the hearthstone of the long house and wept. Their tears welled and felled. Their Waters slithered into the stone as their givers chanted dreams and ancient songs just above a whisper that even I do not remember.

I want to remember, do you believe me?

I have tried to will them up into my heart once again.

I tried to hold them for you.

But I have been unable to awaken the sleeping medicine.

There are certain deaths that can only live once. Certain moments that, if revived, carry only blackness beyond the falling darkness of death.

Such was the life of the boy. When it was over, it was over. In some sense.

But not all, of course.

Their burial songs ushered ancestors and ancient spirits in the smoke of juniper and wort, and they danced silently in the darkness. The bird that nested in the ceiling, in the cruck blade of the timber-framed hall, watched silently.

"What rises without birth, sets without death, is perfectly silent, but walks the loudest?" the Old Mother riddled against the dark of the greying hall and as the juniper bundles' smoke filtered up and then yawned out.

The People were silent, for the Old Mother was known for her guile, and this wouldn't be the first time they would be tricked by her wile.

"What lives without life, dies without death, is wonderfully nothing, and yet is everything?" Bacharigu asked back, her eyes fully glinting the light of the bundles' small flame upon the tear-water-soaked stone.

All the Mothers then smiled and looked into one another, laughing exhaled breath.

No one else dared to answer.

Miach's grave was simple, for medicine carriers would not find new life in this world.

This was their medicine: when taken it would heal but it could not be taken twice.

When he was laid to rest, when they placed the great hearthstone over his body, he would never be seen again.

Not as a boy, at least.

Not long after the ceremony that celebrated Miach's life was complete, and The People stumbled back into the corners of the hall or outside under its eaves to huddle for heat, a certain flower arose from the tear-water-soaked stone.

It rose with silvery breath and pulsating growth.

Then, in the rising light of the early morning, many more sprouted behind it.

By dawn, the stone donned a duvet of flowers.

———————

In the dim and dusking light of the hall, the smoke of juniper foxtrotting around his head, Long-Arm sat still and stared blankly at the stone. He was uncomfortable in the hall yet was warmed by some other memory. His heart was busy replaying the moments living just before his brother's death, over and over again.

His brother's eyes looking into Teyrnon's; his swift scurrying speed in battle; the boy-king's arm motionless at his feet; his back arching and fingers curling under the strange energy; the spear; the blood; the end; the smile in the dust.

Miach's life flashed in front of Long-Arm and he thought he saw the stone pulse from the corner of his eye. He thought he saw its rise and fall, like breath. But the stone was obscured just enough in the darkness to be fully believable and yet entirely improbable. He looked again. The stone once more seemed to pulse.

It shivered like growing heat. It breathed like a belly. Long-Arm was sure of it. He wanted to be sure of it. And so he smiled and then walked out and away with the rising smoke, over their village and beyond.

His brother was there, where he should be, in the long house.

His brother was now a flower.

"What do we know of these flowers?" Long-Arm inquired as he walked, once again, through the yawning doors the following morning. There was a skip in his step and an anchoring hope carried him there.

"We only know what they tell us," the oldest of The Children of Cécht returned, looking up, "and these flowers tell us they grow well on Mountain stone. That is good enough for us. If they say it is true, then it is true. We have no grounds to argue with them," they smirked into a smile like one who laughs at their own joke.

"Are they growing out of—" Long-Arm's voice trailed off as the last word galloped like a band of horses out of the hall and over the plain below that looked awfully like an outstretched arm pointing to the hearthstone. The echo of his question bounced upon the stone and juggled the exploding dust and settled ash into specks of starlight that sparkled around the knees of The Children.

The riddling stars enraptured the room's attention for many moments, the exact amount was unknown, and the silence felt good—

or good enough. Complete and yet moving. Mourning the end but harvesting once again.

"They are not common, even upon the Mountain," one of The Children spoke, breaking the silence. "They call themselves saxifrage, and we see them as a white encrusted yellow flower that, when consumed fresh, relieves paralysis of the tongue."

"Funny this, if it is true. Don't you think?" Long-Arm replied.

"It is true. But we do not think," The Children whispered back, their hands once again focused on their work. As though an aside, they said, "It is not common to see you here. What brings you?"

"The days are lonely," the boy answered quietly. He was looking down and kicking playfully with a stone that did not exist.

"Lonely?" they asked.

"Miach is gone and no longer walks with me. Pryderi took Teyrnon beyond the Mountain for safety. They have not yet returned."

"And neither will they, we think. Their work here, upon this Land, is complete."

"You think? I thought you didn't think." The boy's head turned ever so slightly and strained his neck under the subtle irony.

"We think many things. But never are our thoughts concerned with flowers, for never are flowers concerned with thinking about us."

"Why do you think they won't come back?" the boy asked, now stepping toward the floral hearthstone and selectively picking which topic he would focus on.

"Flowers think not of herbalists because flowers are beautiful," one of The Children returned, ignoring Long-Arm's question.

"And we think not of flowers because we are also beautiful," another of The Children added. "We are beauty in the way that they are beautiful, and they are beauty in the way that we are beautiful. We share in the beauty of this world because we share the world. And we share the world because we are."

"We are what?" Long-Arm questioned incuriously.

"The world," they all returned in chorus.

The oldest of The Children then stepped forward, a step and no more, as though indicating the truth of their words required movement, and said, "When one strips away the beautiful for the practical, the mysterious for the real, when one thinks and does not feel, the melody collapses into discordance and beauty becomes an item to think about."

"What should it be?" the boy asked.

"Someone, I guess, if I were to think about it."

"Do you?"

"Do we what?"

"Want to think about it?"

"No," the oldest of The Children responded, smiling and stepping back into their work behind the table.

———

"A long time ago, it is said—" Long-Arm supposed with his fingers first, breaking the long silence that lived between him and the working Children under the beams of the long house.

"'A long time ago' is not a phrase that is welcome here," they responded in a hasty chorus.

The Children did not look up. Instead, they worked the morning's herbs in the usual and practiced way: first, breaking leaf and blade without severing its connection with the main stem, and then, gently, brocading the naked bases into a strong bundle to dry, minimally, before burning, only slightly, in cold smoke.

They continued, "'A long time ago' is not another place or another time, but a ghost, a tawdry repetition of the ancient pouring like flame over oak or wind over leaf into the present. But she is never let to be the present herself. She is fantasy. Nothing more."

"What is the present, then?" Long-Arm inquired.

"The present is the past and future. The past is the future, just not yet. And the future is the present playing with the past. They are all fine in their own way. As long as they live and are let to live. But 'a long time ago' is just the past, a fantasy of the lonely and desolate."

"Well, it is said then," Long-Arm continued, irritably, and with his finger still playing in the air, "that we once heard the Harp's music everywhere—in the songs of birds, in the flow of Waters from her deep earthen wells, in the ripple of riveting winds lifting leaves, upon the plain as it bounced on the pillars and galloped like the mare under innumerable rays of the world's yellowing light."

"Yes, it was romantic and it was music seen and held by all, everyone, in colors beyond symbols and words," the oldest of The Children remarked.

"All of us, the Oceaners claimed—I think it was their Breoch—" the boy continued, "desire the same thing: order over chaos and the power to wield both. That is to say, avarice."

"We hold that as untrue," the oldest of The Children replied, gratingly, as though it was Long-Arm's thought or in the carrying of the thought, the thought's evil was let to live and must then be then put to death.

After a pause, a long inhale, another of The Children said, "We don't feel that this lives well in the world of many colors, the Land under the Rim."

"Then where does it live?" the boy asked.

"They took it, the Harp—" the oldest of The Children spoke, but with her hand now empty and pointing to the equally empty corner of the hall, "because they have never met a flower. That is why they think the way they do. That is why their eyes are closed. Does a world exist beyond the Rim without flowers?"

"I would imagine anything could exist," the boy thought out loud.

"Then it would be there."

"A real world of real things?"

"Yes, a world without music and a world without mystery."

"How does life live in such a world?"

"It doesn't," the oldest of The Children said, "Life has many mockeries and fake substitutes." Her hands once again green under folding herbs.

Long-Arm stepped forward to the hearthstone. His fingers found a flower and its dawdling petal extending from the dark womb. He imagined its colors flowing like Water and its rivers through his veins until his whole body spiraled into an eddy of color. The aroma of the meadow alighting in smiles only Miach could muster, and he felt warm. It was a natural warmth, but not a warmth he had ever experienced in the dark of the long house. He shivered in response, and he found himself smiling, finally, at the stone.

His fingers, still on the flower, worked loose, gently of course, a particular petal and lifted its falling listlessness, gently of course, to his nose. He felt the soft gauze of the white wing tickle his upper lip. Emotions ran down in energy that lifted the light hairs of his back. The same energy that animated Miach at his life's end.

Salt water surged through his sinuses. He cried.

"Thank you, my brother. My friend," he thought without intention. He thought without sound. He smelled the flower's fragrance as it wafted into his heart, and he saw Miach's apothecary and the alchemy that his life sought. He saw their days pile up like leaves on the forest floor in the spring. Not dead, just becoming else.

"My friend," he thought out loud. "My friend, you were stronger than me, you always were. Oh, how I need you now." Long-Arm, the younger and weaker brother, cried. He was finally finding strength.

———

"When we come together, we worship beauty for its own sake, the many notes adorning the music with theme," The Children interrupted his flowered and familial dream after a distended moment.

"It is here," the oldest of The Children said as she lifted her hand and placed it over her heart and then tapped it down into her stomach, finger walking over finger. "Harmony sinks to fill the deepest of depths and rises to the highest of heights. Here," again tapping her stomach, "together, we resonate."

"That feels good, thank you." Long-Arm was not looking. His fingers were now deep and rooting in their own work with Miach's flowers. His tongue, the first organ of this resonance, was relieved of any paralysis. But something bound him in place, some unimaginable and intangible force blurred the barrier between him and the stone, and, for the moment, he felt Miach with them, with him, and he felt the warmth that his brother's care often provided.

"They are here to make the unknown known, the uncommon plain, aren't they?" he asked after a pause.

"Yes, they are here to make the plain a pond."

"To speak unbelonging. Why?"

"Because they don't belong," the oldest of The Children replied. "When times are urgent, we do not speed up but slow down. The way we respond to crisis must not be to add to the crisis. As a people, we are not about solutions or answers, but creativity, questions, inquiry, and not knowing."

"Not knowing what?"

"Experts are like wind in the willows. Gentle and shy, they are beautiful. Aggressive, they limit the utter creativity of the world and destroy her."

"Are you saying that the Oceaners are experts?"

"No, but they are like experts in that they don't belong," the oldest of The Children continued, laughing subtly. "To them, our belonging is savage, undeveloped. It insults them. It is an insult to them. As long as we exist, they are reminded that they do not." At this, she rolled up her sleeve, a repetition revealing her elbow, and she fell back into her work.

Her eyebrows were so extraordinarily thick with green vines and twirling shiny leaves that they seemed ready to leap, a curl twisting and reaching for response. The boy had never noticed this before, but the light was growing, and the light played with the long house in strange ways.

"Listen to the voices that still the torrent. Those that only peace can hear," he heard a whicker from the herbalist's table, the source of the words, the speaker, unknown and purposefully so. He looked away and felt free. Free to move, free to run, free to find his life. He looked away.

The dawn of the day proceeded through the wooden window frames, and the shadows elongated fast, veiling the boiling colors of the garden lantern light and clothing the herbalists in their work under yellow and pink corrals of color. The way the soft light gleamed against the dark interior was new and altogether magikal, like the searching fingers of the soft breeze through a kissing canopy of trees.

Walking away, he pivoted and looked back. His eyes found The Children bent over their oak-hewn table, and he noticed something that he did not recognize before. The slanting window light shone strangely upon the form and allowed his attention to focus on it for the first time. There was a glowing ember wrapped in a mat of moist river reeds on the table, exhaling a small black smoke.

"Since Pryderi is gone," The Children said, feeling the boy's glare, sensing his sight.

"You are preserving the fire?" Long-Arm asked.

They did not respond. They did not need to.

After a long moment, time bloating now under the light smoke of the glowing ember, with hands deep into the medicine, the oldest of The Children muttered, "The dawn is here, but death beats at the door. We are coming to an end. Walk with death, Long-Arm. Miach slumbers but does not sleep, for the fire yet lives."

"Who's end?" he asked irately. "Who's end is coming?" he demanded immediately. His words followed the cadence of his beating heart—fast and sharp and becoming only faster—but were strong and stronger than he expected.

But his question only beckoned against pulsing stone.

The Children never answered.

They would never answer.

Later that morning.

*O*ne is quick to find a limit, I like to say, when considering a small aspect of something larger, of something monumentally innumerable.

Like Earth.

Like love.

Limits are strange things: the more you test them, the more they test you back. You can say what you like about philosophy, but it is of little value and of even less worth when it attempts to understand limits.

This is the wisdom of the Raven, but you don't have to listen, for I am only a bird.

I offer this to you as a gift: break through the limit, and you will find another affronting you, and the more limits you break, the closer they will become.

Limits are living.

There is no other way about it.

They walk like you and fly like me.
But they are more forgiving.
I am not. Forgiving.
You will see.
One has only to look to see the white rising behind them, of all the colors and music at once, for their thoughts, and at times they themselves, to want to run in a panic—in part from the imagined size of the growing mass and in part from its perceived effects.
The very act of observation changes everything.
The madness of the world (yours, not ours) colonizes from the outside in. It removes observation and then, ultimately, acknowledgment.
Loneliness is dissonance through desolation. It colonizes as it goes. It walks like limits but unnatural like sand rippling over water.
To colonize, one must separate. To be colonized, we must become desolate—uninhabited, a cage of bones without a rapping heart or a beating life.
The Oceaners took our colors. Worse, they made them their own.
That is the story I have told you.
Slowly, they denuded the world within the Rim and offered no hospitality in return.
This is the story we have shared.
Then, they stole the music and killed the medicine.
I have also now told you this story.
But today, the day of days, they will empty our world and bleed us dry. Today, desolation will attempt to reign over the ponding plain.
This came next.

The Sun shone brightly upon the smooth sward shoveling down on all sides that skewered the village atop an island in the plain. Dales and falling glens climbed higher into the upland hills below the great arm of the Mountain to find safety and reprieve. To find someplace dry. The Water growing, the pond climbing behind the Land, reaching for her, and gaining ground.

"Alas! I fear our dawdling has come to an end," said Balor. He looked toward the rising Waters encircling the village and smiled.

At the head of the valley, miles distant but shining brightly, a torrent spun like silver webs over an endless ladder of short waterfalls. The Waters, rushing rudely, were paving their own streams and rivers, their own meanders and putrid oxbow lakes. A mist, rising and circling when it rose, hung in the air until it vanished above the Mountain's feet. The bog's birds and curlews were gone. The meadow's larks and swallows, her hares and foxes, had long ago run together into the scared uplands, putting aside their differences. The Land was deaf but also deafening, quiet yet torrential.

"Beyond this Land rushes the Waters that work their way hither. Yonder, the cruel other, the tumbling current, is constant and coming close," Balor said as a tremor circulated through his spectating soldiers.

He turned to his men. "Their end is nigh! We have leveled their tents and reduced their identities, their individuality, into a singular mob." He then turned to Breoch, his gaze leveling upon the boy-king's unbalanced body. "But they still have hope. No! They had hope. Today, we will rip the mob into factions, their stone circles into glass shards. Today, they will walk alone, or drown."

At this, another tremor ricocheted through Balor's men and quivered over the Land as a winded and black gale, lifting leaves and falling trees. It found the fire's forgotten ash and twisted the white memories of the ancient village into a ripping red tornado. It laughed as it denuded the landscape, and the Oceaners tittered behind it.

"Bring me the village," Balor commanded.

And so they did.

—————

Balor's attendants chortled as they gathered The People into a vile pantomime.

They ripped the herbalists from the long house, dragging them by their red hair. Their feet kicked new rivers in the dust. The Oceaners then encircled the rest of the village around the fire-blackened and open-aired hearth that smelled of charred leather and sallow hair follicles.

A deep, sombre breath saturated the lungs of the Land as the Síraide released all hope in a single exhale. Some fell to their knees and wailed. Others, only few, stood with stern façades—and façades they were, for any hope held at this moment was artificial light. It was about to be turned off at the source.

Balor then strung The Children together like bundles of sage and placed a mockery of flame at their feet.

"Dance!" Breoch screamed, his eyes now blood black. His veins bulging, swollen and sullen under his young face's perfect skin. He wore the expression of one lacking honor. "Smoke!" He screamed. "Purify us!" He mocked.

"Oh! You flowers of the field! Oh! Your purple feathered spears, clean us! Cleanse us, oh! You gods of sage!" other Oceaners muttered and mocked.

A brackish dust steadily rose from the burnt circle like an overturned ocean floor as the herbalists' unshod feet slapped and tapped a false rhythm. Waterless tears fell from their eyes—a mourning buffeted with only their bodies' salt. Sadness triumphing. Sadness winning. It was as though they knew this was their end's beginning. And if they did, then they were correct.

They at first tried their best, but the tight rope that was tied about them soon frayed the fabrics of their patience, and their feet dawdled the dance into an ungentle strut like a child dragging their feet on a long walk.

"Dance!" the Oceaners screamed and mocked.

"Smoke! Burn and cleanse us!" Breoch again chimed a chortle in the squealing chaos. He bent and set actual flame to the bundles.

Screams wailed from The People, who were still formed in a circle and held back by a speared network of Oceaner soldiers. Cries carried the dust back down, and some of them even burst through the soldiers' barricade to help the now burning Children. But they were beat down, immediately, and dragged back to the circle's rim by their hair.

Hope appeared to be lost.

The fire at the herbalists' feet grew unnaturally, itself finding a strange fuel in the drifting dust. It seared the unwoven hems of their long tunics. Tattered strings loosed and threadbare in time burned first and caused the initial slapping and the tapping to progress finally into jumping, as a peculiar smoke, not entirely unlike sage, rose around them. It covered them, the dust and the smoke, and it clothed their cries in a desert black.

The only positive was that the smoke pushed the dust down. The only negative was that they were on fire.

Long-Arm's eyes burned as The Children of Cécht screamed and danced. Smells, like putrid flesh but flowery, exploded above him like innumerable spores from tiny mushrooms. But poisonous and poisoning. A black haze fluttered and flew. A maddened laughter called it back down, the thick soot of smoke bending and waving in Breoch's hand.

Long-Arm's anger burned. He closed his fists, and they found a firm white that welled from a hate hitherto unknown. At first, it was sadness—the ponding below in the plain, the loss of their identity, their sovereignty, Miach's death. Now, the sadness mocked from the inside, and a strong anger welled to replace the distance of his thoughts with immediacy.

He jumped forward and tried to advance, to help, but his screaming body found the tip of an Oceaner's spear keeping the circle clear. It pressed into his chest and cut a slim slit just under his collar. A drop of blood coagulated to close the linen.

Breoch then dragged the Old Mother from her place behind the tormented and wailing and screaming mass and into the heart of the circle. Her feet landed a foot beyond the herbalists' dancing flame, and its red-yellow-orange-blue light faded against the white in her eyes. The fire dwindled as though an invisible rain calmed the flame.

"She is consuming the fire," Long-Arm thought to himself. The hope in his chest rising, his heart beating wilder, for the moment.

"No, she is becoming it," Bacharigu said from her position next to him, listening to his thoughts. He had not previously noticed that she was there, in the circle, let alone standing next to him. But it was not her presence that startled him. It was her words—her knowledge of his thoughts, that woke him with a white snap.

The Old Mother's litheness impressed both the Oceaners and the Síraide. She was older than the Star Oak, and it was said, although only a few still believed, that she held the Harp when it was first given to us. She was impossibly ancient, and the particular impossibility of what came next was what made the moment tangible for all to see.

"She is as old as the river," Long-Arm thought, again to himself.

"She is the river," Bacharigu returned with a wink.

Their eyes met and welled together in tears. And for a moment, all was white. For a moment, all was calm and clear, a Kinship cresting like light frost over the once dew dappled leaves of the meadow's many flowers. He recognized her, and while he did not know what the moment held, he felt sure that she was a central aspect of it.

But Breoch screamed and interrupted, "You! The Mother of the meadow's wort! You! The Mother of the Waters' well that rivers divert! You, today, The Mother, will fall. You, today, The Mother, we will cull."

Breoch then dropped his hand and his lips fell like eels that slip slowly below the riverbank. Three Oceaner attendants then strode forward and ripped off the Old Mother's clothes in one great and sweeping motion. The strong seams tore streams of blood when they ripped through her skin, and Long-Arm thought he could see a translucent liquid leaking out. The texture and fertility of the plain and its rising woods and rocky uplands seemed to leak out of her. Sweet earth and ancient bog muck in place of blood and offal.

She was in the center of the circle, now standing fully over the flame and looking straight into Breoch. Her face carried no emotion. Not yet. But her body was not naked, not at least in any simple sense. Her clothes were ripped off, yes, but a simple pottery white linen tunic draped around her. It waved in the wind of the flame like a river's current and was adorned with draping reeds and river grasses.

"The river," Long-Arm thought, his head leaning into the blood of the moment, the idea becoming alive and growing legs in his mind and walking, gently, into his heart.

But the cries of the burning Children and the tiring Old Mother crescendoed with the laughter of the Oceaners into a horrid melody, and, looking up, Long-Arm couldn't figure why this great pain fell upon such a brilliant afternoon when the baby blue sky allied herself wonderfully with a mild and gentle heat uncommon for the late season.

So much beauty.

And so much pain.

The rain rising to kiss the sky.

Red hailstones falling in torrents of blood.

Looking down, his eyes caught those of the Old Mother. He looked into them, those orbs shrouded in flame and smoke, those orbs reflecting light. She looked into him and then her eyes darted to the left, to the girl next to him, to Bacharigu. He thought he saw her smile. He thought he saw a word flutter from her mouth to the girl. But he couldn't be sure.

The flame was too much.

Too intense to know anything at all.

Then, behind the flame and obscured by its great smoke, a young girl appeared and stood with the Old Mother.

"In the flame!" he cried out loud. "Where did she come from?" he whispered to himself.

The girl in the flame had hair of red-gold and a coral tunic that extended into a long train behind her. But she did not burn. She was kneeling, or so Long-Arm thought, but he was unsure of what he really could see. She seemed to be holding the Old Mother's hands. They seemed to be looking at each other. The flame's anger wrapped and smacked against their forms, and smoke flit up in deep dark blacks, but they did not burn.

They were sitting with each other now, legs crossed and talking like over tea. The flames lapped and pounded against them. The young woman laughed, and the Old Mother giggled a response.

They were beautiful.

They were beauty itself.

At this, a great wind rose from the west and carried the winter with it. A torrent of rain fell, and Long-Arm saw each drop fall as faceted jewels reflecting the swelling and final light of the fire.

The wind became alive. It was colored somewhere between ocean Water and the swelling wells of the river Cailleach. It carried, as it entered the circle, the smell of marsh reeds and soused grasses from beyond the village that once wafted and rode over the plain. It carried the colors of the curlew in flight and the welter and smudging waste of the ocean beyond. It was everything all at once.

The wind then wafted up and out, and the rains left with it. Not a moment later, time enough only for Long-Arm's gaze to turn from the plain to the heart of the circle, the Old Mother was once again standing alone in the fire. She flailed and screamed the shrieks of a burning sorceress through blistering flame and dropped into a bundle of rags, trying to hide from the fire or maybe to find a pocket of air.

Everything became brighter. The blue-orange-yellow light illuminating even the darkest spaces. It flickered and flashed. Lapped and laced the sky with uncurling and reaching fingers. The smell of bowels, boiling blood, and charred flesh wrapped like ancient moss around stone, and she stood up. Impossibly, she stood up and looked at Breoch.

She said, "The evil see evil in this world. But that does not make the world evil." Then, after a shallow inhale, she riddled, "What rises without birth?"

A smirk scythed across her lips. Then flame, so much flame. Her teeth biting the flame, the flame biting them back.

Bacharigu, now once again standing beside Long-Arm, returned just above a whisper, "And what lives without life?"

Their eyes, the Old Mother and hers, together conjoined in tears as they flitted fresh spring Water upon the burning dust. The girl's breath smelled like herbs steeped in hot Water. The pale and ageless burning form of the Old Mother then shot a sparkling star into the sky and was no more. The smile, the tear, her last word.

The fire then burned the dust and settled slowly. Around the circle, The People were patting the bundles of herbalists out. In an instant, the chaos fell into numb panic.

Breoch, perched above it all, smiled as the mayhem fell and stilled like ash. A Raven flew overhead and cast a shadow dapple. Long-Arm looked around. The girl, Bacharigu, was gone.

A great wailing cry was all that remained.

"The madness of your world creeps like an illness in the dark," Breoch spoke after a long pause, smiling like one who pissed in the mead. "It reeks an inhabiting desolation, an illness with tendrils like roots. Better for us to become a wave. Today, your champions will be my servants, your bards will carry my firewood, and your dreamers will be my rath-builders."

Even more wailing rose with the falling smoke.

He continued, "Today, you will become our reality, and Ogham, your language, will be forgotten. Naming is a powerful thing. Names allow the wielding to control. This is the power I seek. This is the power the Land gave to me when I took it from her. You will no longer live as one people. Bereft, you will live lonelily and in our way."

At this, his many attendants fell upon The People and separated them, chaining them to hard labor and chaining them, also, from each other.

"But this is not the fullness of our day's work," Breoch interrupted with another chortle. "We have one last task for you."

Breoch looked at Balor, and then his eyes fell back on the dawdling flame at the center of the circle. His eyes seemed concerned with the pile of pottery white rags crumbling into even whiter ash.

"Today," he continued without looking away from the rags, "the boy will fall the *Máithrín*. Today, your world will end."

The next day, following the burning of the Old Mother, but now high on the bald Mountain.

H ello," the tree said to the boy.

"Hello," the boy returned.

"Why are you here?"

"I have cause for it." Long-Arm was looking away. His eyes scudded down the Mountain and splashed into the plain below. He watched as the camp's smoke filtered above an unnatural hearth. The chimneys were quiet. There was no food lapped by flame.

"On summer's eve," the boy said just above a whisper when the day's growing darkness began to settle, "we sit and watch the Sun's set reflect against you, and on the summer's morn', we watch her burn you alive."

"An enflamed sacrifice to the gods, no?" the tree responded, laughing to herself as she remembered the mare and the mugwort's words.

"No. To her friends." The boy smirked slyly and then was silent.

"Every thought is but an echo," the tree said, ignoring the empty space between them.

"An echo?" the boy questioned without returning his gaze.

"An echo."

"And? I am sure—"

"And," the tree continued, talking over him, "every thought is but an echo of words cast before, don't you think?"

"I try not to think," the boy replied, remembering his conversation with The Children in the long house.

"Good. That is good," the tree smiled, and a shiver wiggled up her trunk and animated the lowest limb, sparking her amber autumn leaves into a living green once again.

The boy smiled but kept his gaze in the valley. It was not good. This whole affair did not feel good.

He found it difficult to look upon the tree, to place his eyes on her. Those orbs who would watch her die. Those who will cast the final blow.

He felt the hickory handle of the axe mottle a pale pink in his left hand. He felt the shame rising. He felt his heart falling. His breath smashed somewhere in between.

Gasping for air, his lungs screamed. Turning pale, his heart ripped through its sack and robbed the verve from his veins. He stood there on the bald Mountain with his head down.

"When we listen and when we love," the tree said, "when we work and when we fight, we allow others to carry our soul."

"That is what I am told—no one moves alone," the boy returned.

"What do you mean, alone?" the tree questioned.

"Solu—"

At this, and before his mouth formed the last hissing syllable, a great shiver rumbled like thunder from below his feet and burst like the river's bank over the landscape and its dusk-downed grasses. Colors of red and reddening blacks shivered like shook dust in the air about him. He felt their sparkle like little spears puncturing his skin. Pinpricks of bulging blood like dewdrops. Petite worlds of clabbered orbs fell into a fine curdle, feeling their way out, falling their way down.

Then, silence. Everything and its everyone fell calm once again.

"Do not use that language here!" retorted the tree with a voice that was ushered from limb and branch and even, it seemed, from the ivy veiling her boughs.

The boy shuddered and stepped back. A fear otherwise unshared echoed through him, unnaturally like a spear but sharper.

"What language?" he asked shyly but with a prosaic tepidness.

"The Oceaner's tongue," the tree replied, "their language speak is not welcome upon this Land."

"It is they who have sent me," the boy admitted, tasting the confession leave his mouth. He blushed under its empty heaviness.

"No, it is not they who carry their souls."

"How do you mean?"

"They carry a dissonance for desolation," said the tree, "a worldview replacing a worldsense, if you understand."

"I don't," the boy replied. His expression pursed.

"Worldview is belief crafted from one's conception of what they see," the tree explained. "It is built from and constructs the fundamental aspects of reality. Some may even go so far as to assert that your worldview is your search for meaning, its underlayment of purpose, and the values you erect as fundamental to this fabricated life."

"Okay, a worldview is the essence behind one's beliefs?" the boy asked.

"Fine. That is good enough."

"And if that is held here," he motioned with one of his hands, indicating the polarity, "then what is the other? This worldsense as you speak?"

"There is no polarity. There are no hands about it." The tree interrupted his question. "This is not a counting game or a life where that which is not good cannot be redeemed when it walks astride the good, or, better still, as the good."

"I don't follow," the boy blushed.

"What is dissonance?"

"Well, I figure it is a lack of harmony. Atonality."

"Good. And what if that which is atonal harmonizes with itself?"

The boy paused, a swell of angst rising into the space left by his heart only moments before. He asked the question to himself, repeating it. Soon, not long, he said, "Then, I would think it would not be dissonant."

"Good. Very good. And so what is dissonance?"

"I don't know—I—"

"—Keep searching. Close your eyes. Feel." The tree seemed to close the space between them, her questions searching the space for his heart-mind's solution.

"Well," the boy said squinting, scared to commit, "it is atonality viewed from only one perspective. Or, really, it is the music's melody for only one purpose."

"Good. Very good! This tastes like spring wind. I often wonder about spring winds—where do they come from?"

"I have never thought about that."

"You have never thought about it? That is strange."

"I don't think that is strange," he said.

"Why?"

"Because I am not a tree."

"But you are a tree."

"I am?"

"Yes, clearly."

"No, it's not clear."

"But you are talking to one."

"Yes, but that does not make me a tree."

"No?"

"No," he responded with aggravated simplicity, raising his two hands in a swinging motion.

"Put down your arms and let your hands dawdle at your side like branches," the tree returned.

After an uncomfortable pause, uncomfortable only for the boy, the tree continued, "Polarity demands a singular perspective—a worldview. What is infinite appears to be polar when you see it as such. What if harmony's lack, that is, atonality or dissonance, is not blindness but the problem of sight?"

The boy fumbled with the axe in his hand. He again found himself looking down, looking back from whence he came, to the village. His eyes then searched about the heights and dusking mists of the bald Mountain for Miach. He had never ventured this far without his brother. He was uncomfortable and growing more so.

"If you cannot answer that question, let me ask another—what is the limit?" the tree asked.

"I don't understand," the boy returned.

"If one's worldview is value created from what you see, then what is the limit of what one values?"

"Well, it would be what one can see."

"Yes, perfect. That is fine. Value, in this way, is created and maintained by only one of your senses. Is value something we create or does it have a finer root elsewhere?"

"I would imagine you believe it has deep roots but not roots preserved by one tree alone," the boy returned, standing taller now, becoming more comfortable.

The tree settled back, lifting a limb to fall down slightly with a shiver of a shake. She seemed to wait, patiently, for Long-Arm's mind to play with the thoughts, with the feelings of this strange and unexpected conversation.

"Let me get this right," he continued after a short while, "you are saying that the idea of a worldview makes relative that which is universal because it places the idea of tonality in the eyes, in only that which we can see? And, this singular perspective," he thought out loud, "constructs a world of binary minds, seeking binary values, where members become poles and not relatives?"

"Good. And so, are you a tree?"

"I see what you are doing," the boy said, unsure if he was supposed to smile or not.

"Or do you smell it?" she laughed loudly.

His blood was catching up to the Mountain's music. His stomach ushering a short utterance of exhaled breath. He laughed. It was the color of her cambium—light green and paling in the autumn.

"But do you feel it?" the tree spoke lightheartedly.

The boy's smile matured into a crescendo.

They smiled.

Together.

"Are you ready to continue?" the tree asked after a long pause that traced the falling Sun many degrees in his motion.

"I guess, but I am not here to—"

"A worldsense is like a worldview but more whole, more living, more animistically colorful and beautiful," she said without attending to his concerns. "A worldsense is mystery felt and never knowledge held."

"A worldsense, yes, but—" he said, hearing the words fall from his lips while also trying to stall the conversation.

"How many sounds exist in nature?" she asked, again dismissing his concerns outright.

The boy's rising temper stilled curiously. He then placed a finger on his lips, feeling the calloused coarseness, the undulating rivulets of his essence that swirl and eddy around imaginary pillars.

"They are infinite, I would imagine," he said.

"Good. If all music is good enough for the birds shining love upon the wind, the babbling brooks bursting silvery tremors upon their shifting banks, and the drumming hooves that clamor a turbulence of dust upon the plain, then why aren't they good enough for you?"

"I never said they weren't," he replied.

"Yes, you did," she said.

"How?"

"You said it was *their* atonality that sent you."

"Yes."

"So did they?"

"Did they what?" the boy asked, cross and growing more so.

"Send you."

"I guess?"

"Or do you know?"

"I believe."

"You do not believe. Neither do you guess. You know. And, if you know, then you do not believe that all music is good," she said sternly.

The boy stood in silence. He stood without knowing if he stood at all.

The sky was paling now into the day's final moments and Long-Arm thanked the darkness for its shadow, its concealment. The ground below his feet felt unstable. He had ventured long into the sacred and scared uplands and summited the bald Mountain in order to fall the tree. A ghastly act of heresy, he knew it to be. An act of the enslaved soul, the denuded life. The forced hand, drawn but never open.

The Oceaners demanded it to be done, and they demanded the work's completion by nightfall. If he failed, Breoch told him, they would all be cut down and burned, one by one. If he failed, their colonization would heighten into unfathomable depths—depths that would destroy The People for good, depths that would drown the plain until it was remembered only as an ocean.

"Darkness is light shared. Night is the day on lend," the tree said after a good while of dusking silence that screamed like a drowning choir.

"I came here alone. I am alone to blame." Long-Arm said. His eyes now falling fully into his palms. His fingers finding the hickory handle and again he thought of why he was here. He took the blame, and he found satisfaction in finding a firm hold in something.

"So, you came up here by yourself?" the tree asked.

"Yes," the boy returned.

"You journeyed here on your own?"

"Yes," the boy again spoke without energy and with speech boring into dullness like an auger.

"And you arrived without anyone else?"

"Yes."

"Alone?"

"Yes"

"No!" the tree screamed with a newly awakened energy. Her leaves shook, and she dropped a perfectly hewn red-orange leaf that danced and twisted and then landed in his palm.

He looked away. But he did not let the leaf fall.

After an extruded moment, she continued, "The journey is not about arriving, and if it is not about arriving, then the journey is about something much deeper, don't you think?"

"Do you want me to think?" he asked.

A subtle smile smirked in the corner of his upper lip and caused a squint, if only barely, in the eyes resting above.

"Do you know what the journey is about?" the tree asked.

"No, but it seems like you do," the boy said, shifting.

"I know many things. But I think about very few of them. There is little worthy of thinking over. But I feel everything."

She paused and gathered her leaves about her. Her great limbs shook and shivered like a bird's feathers after the rain. A late swallow lifted from one of her yet green branches and flitted outward, following an invisible veil of smoke that trailed southward.

"I came alone," the boy said, his eyes following the black feathers.

"No, you arrived alone. Or, really, you arrived as who you were meant to be," the tree returned. "If you are the music, if you are the medicine wrapped in a beautiful melody, how can you be anything else?" Another shiver pulsed through her. "Be you, my friend, my boy," she said, smiling greatly.

"They are trying to separate us, isolate and desolate us," the boy said in a copse of panic. It grew from his gut and it grew erroneously large in that instant. He was shaking and shifting, and if it wasn't for the axe in his hands, he would have thought that he was dreaming in deep visions.

"No, they are making you think that you are lonely."

"Like I am now. Alone?" he asked, now shaking.

"No, those who wonder are never lonely. And those who wander together will always be, in time, fully alone."

"I don't understand," the boy said.

"Do you want to understand?" she asked.

"I don't know," the boy responded.

"Let me help you. Where did understanding evade you?"

"I guess I am confused—what is the difference between being alone and being lonely?"

"Ah, yes," the tree returned with a smile that broke the chipping white bark that was reminiscent of the white oak. "I am glad you asked. To be alone, one has only to find themselves naked and unafraid."

"Courageous?" the boy asked.

"No, fearless," the tree returned. "And when you become fearless, you may also find yourself contained in the great and woven fabric of life, of dreaming and walking those dreams."

"Okay, but what is loneliness?" the boy asked.

"Isolation," she said simply. "Isolated, you began your journey, but alone, you summited my mount," the tree said. "Remember, worldview and worldsense. You may view yourself as lonely but you, in fact, in wandering here, became alone. When you become fearless, you become whole, and without fear, you become wholly alone because you become wholly you."

"What about listening and loving and working and fighting and others carrying my soul?" Long-Arm asked, confused. Hysteria and overwhelm settling not so subtly upon his chest and rising into a cheeky blush.

"*Your* soul. Singular. To be alone does not mean you aren't carried. A great fabric, warp and weft, brocaded in the meadow's silk, requires the singular thread, and she requires the woven strength of the weave. You can see the single thread or you can see the weave. I am asking you to see her. The all of her," the tree said simply and with a simplicity that smelled like confusion.

————————

"Why are you here?" Her countenance shifted into a new color as if waking from a dream.

Long-Arm stumbled back and once again found the sharpened steel in his hand. The silvery cold biting through the handle into his veins. He remembered Breoch's command biting through his skin like worms in the wrong direction.

"I don't know anymore," Long-Arm admitted. He was blushed and blushing. His blood was rising and also, strangely, very thin. Lightheaded, nearly.

"Surely, you need something. Ask me—what do you need?" the tree asked.

"Our resource allocations have dwindled of late. They have come to take what is left."

"Oh! You have come for my lumber?" the tree inquired, shivering a branch that grew weft and parallel to the bald Mountain. A tree itself, the sizeable arm then shattered cleanly at its base upon the north end of the tree and collided in a great rippling splash upon the Land.

"There, that is good. I give this of me for you. Go in peace."

"I can't," Long-Arm returned, shifting his feet in the oak-wave dancing grasses.

"Why?"

"I—I need more."

"You need more?" the tree questioned, the sap welling into a waterfall of tears from the broken limb.

"Yes," he said in a whisper.

"Why?"

"I told you," Long-Arm said with his hand circling the space, "You will fetch a good price beyond the Rim of our world."

"What is 'price?'"

"Money, I would imagine. The Oceaners require it."

"Oh! So they need money to live?"

"That is the law of the Oceaners."

"What does it taste like? I have never had this money."

"What does what taste like?"

"Money. That which my limbs fetch beyond the Rim of the world."

"No. They don't eat the money but use the money to buy what they eat."

At this, a great wind rose from the plain below, and a deep shudder of a quake released a great multitude of acorns from the branches of the great oak. The boy stumbled back to avoid being pelted by the deluge.

"There, that is good. I give this of me for you. Go in peace."

"I can't," he said, bending down to pick up an oak nut and finding a million to choose from.

"Why?"

"I—I need more," he said, with words faltering behind falling tears. His culpability welling in Waters.

"I understand," the tree said simply.

That was it. That was everything, and that was enough.

It is a strange thing to see—the silent gift of a tree.

Her bark cleft just below the lowest branch, and her face fell inward like a winding wave eating itself or like a soul finding fruition.

Her sweeping beard of unshaven ivy dangled listlessly. The soft warm wind played in her canopy like a lover, twisting each curl, gently and equally and with equal measure.

It seemed to be calling her home. The wind.

But home to where?

Breath is that which rises but is never born and falls but never dies.

It is the life that never lives.

Long-Arm stepped forward, his feet ambling over acorns and his fingers finding their work in the darkness.

"I am sorry," his heart said as it rose vertebral into his chest and pulsed a mournful energy through his veins.

"No," a sound screamed like a granite cliff with only a flaming grey sky beyond. "Do not apologize. This is good. I give this of me for you," the faceless tree echoed, its bark wrinkling into a westerly wind.

"Long ago and also today," the tree, the falling *Máithrín*, the great oak and creator of all life that sits atop the bald Mountain above the plain of the Síraide, continued, "before the first muck mired into mist, before the first lit of the curlew lifted in a whistling second rise, before the Horse carried mankind in her yellowing mane, before the

Mountain and the *Fáil* stone cast her melody upon the formless deep and ageless heights—I was.

"When the music asked for harmony, I gave you the Harp from the sinew of my southern branch. When the plain asked for pillars, I gave you resonance, that is life, from the cambium of my own crown. When the resonance asked for a reliquary, I gave you the long house from the hewn planks of my western reach. The music creates, the pillars live, and the reliquary's medicine supplies your rebirth.

"And now, I will give you what you ask for," she said as tears like raining dew fell upon the boy. "In response, I ask for only one thing, a gift for the last and final moment of this old tree: you will erect a tomb of passage next to the river. Deep inside, on the black back wall of the chamber, you will construct a symbol in the darkness. The great tomb will catch the rising Sun on the shortest day of the year, my day, the day of death, a time of renewal and lengthening days born once again, and the chamber will trap our star's loving light high in the ceiling above. On this day, and for only one moment, the stones inside will shine the color of the cloud-spat morning and will certainly reflect this warmth upon the hidden symbol."

"What symbol do you see?" Long-Arm asked, crying uncontrollably. Pulled into the question by some force. His face falling fully into tears as his arms wailed the axe upon her. Steel biting her silver skin. He worked and he listened.

"You will spin three circles upon each other to indicate my three gifts. Harmony, resonance, and reliquary. It is there that you will place your dead, and it is there, on the shortest day of the year, I will shine and carry your dead home," she said.

After a short moment, for the boy's axe was deep into her heartwood now, she said as though waking from a dream, "Now, fall fully into your work. I give this of me. For you alone. Let this steel fall fully. Let this steel fully fall. I am ready. I have found peace."

At this, Long-Arm sunk his axe into her final core, the heart of her heartwood, his tears blurring the utter mayhem around him. He swung and screamed. Breath bouncing over the bald heights. He was wild and wildly himself. Yellow mucus mixed with white tears and splattered like blood.

Then, she fell.

The sound of one iron eating into two hearts echoed upon the Mountain like a spring wind and concluded with the dawn.

The Sun rose red.

Three days later.

The boy woke from his dream, writhing his blistered hands before feeling them upon the dirt floor. They stung when feeling returned. They burned when speared with the dust.

He stood. For moments, Long-Arm stood with his feet feeling the sadness felt by his hands only a moment ago. Feelings that feel different when felt through feet, a beatific agony that deforms our planta limbs like great winds and rain deforms our plant cousins. Bleeding time but acquiescing to its flow. Heedless of its pull. Lost in the push.

The events of the previous days tangled with the black sullenness of the room around him. The pitching nadir of the valley below, the chorus of whispering waves of the susurrant sea rising and waiting to crash.

He was unpracticed in the art of papering over pain and he lay for a while, huddled in the darkness, shivering the dawn awake and fumbled to understand, to tease out, the dream from the real: what happened upon the Mountain and what happened next.

That was history now: what the Oceaners did with her wood, how they scraped and smoothed her innumerable layers of curves and knots into finite dimensions, how they sold her without thought to people who would build without kindness.

Long-Arm lay in the oak dust of his work and wouldn't have believed it was all real without the physical reminder of her split oak fibers, years really, coughing through his sinuses. A red hued ochre clotted and choked.

The fire that once alighted the hearth beside him was dead. Even the color of smoke that purled beyond the black was void.

Everything was blackness. Everything was bleak.

A subtle rain drolled like upturned leaves and drummed a grey harshness against the roof of the building. Opening his eyes, he saw her face hovering in the silence. The tree, her spirit, was with him. It was somehow alit, fully alighted from some other source. She looked at him. He looked at her. Two souls chained and caged in the horror. Cramped in the dark room.

The voice, a ghost in the blackness.

"You will spin three circles." The words splashed against the wall and fell into a molding pile of thick red liquid. It coagulated under a torrid mist and then rose like steam into the form of a Raven.

"It is there that you will place your dead," the Raven reminded. She hovered in the blackness. "And I will carry your dead home."

"The Oceaners carry a plague of certainty," the boy replied to the Raven in terror. Or was it the *Máithrín's* ghostly face? Or both?

There was a momentum growing in his voice. A mad tone. Praying for anemia of mind. Memory feverish and becoming fetid in the darkness. An absolution from forgiveness.

Then, an image struck him. Hooves and unshod feet, sparkling blue skies playing with cloud-spat whites and ochre and tawny rays, Pryderi's mane yellowing yet under the enclosing heaven, the ashen Moon so near and white in the day that he could almost drink it dry.

Pryderi nickered as she draught at their favorite spring, its clear Waters falling from her velvet lips.

"Someday, you will enter the long house upon the dusk of a red evening and become who you are. Someday, you will hear your name. Someday you will need mine," the Raven said, or at least seemed to say. But it was dark.

———————

He awoke. He had tossed and turned violently in the sweaty sheets.

He looked to the wall. The red-beaked Raven still hovered above the pool of blood. Awake or otherwise, he saw that she was still here.

They looked at each other, and he was unsure if Pryderi had really been there at all or if it was just the Raven speaking through vision.

"You will need my name," he thought, a peculiar memory arising within him. He saw the girl. The Star Oak. Her feet dangling from the branches. His memory confused but straightening, slowly, in the dark of the room.

Laying under the black of a blacker dawn, everything was tight as though the leathery flesh of their world had been stretched, scraped, and dried taut across the gaps of whitening bone. Like an animal hide drum. There, alongside the tightness, atop the outer fringed edge of the leather, was a peculiar energy, a flowering flitting inward, a rhythm.

He felt as though he had been wrung like muddy marsh water through a milk-white sieve, and everything was clean and becoming clearer. Everything was rising into a new beat. The symbols and stories of his life being knit together into the fabric of his name: Long-Arm.

"To walk over the plain is to walk through scripture," he said out loud, remembering Pryderi's words.

"To find peace upon the plain is to become scripture," the Raven, still floating above him, returned.

Standing up, a strange sense of subtle nausea fell over the boy and toppled him to his knees. He was embalmed by sweat and memory, his heart a spear tipped by the acrid edge of loneliness. He had a name for it now.

Pryderi, the *Máithrín*, the Old Mother, Miach—all gone. Teyrnon as well. The village outside of what he thought was a room was perfectly quiet.

His life seemed to have been woven for this moment but he was unsure as to why. He was unsure of many things.

He looked up, reveling in the animality of it all.

————

Masters must enslave twice.

First, they enclose themselves as chattel of wit and will. Second, their new irons work outward, always outward. Always born from what they have been already consumed by.

Occupation, or its colonization, is not entirely different.

First, it is a mucky smoke.

Second, a glitter of doom.

————

A moment later, the door opened.

Subtle trickles of light filtered through the heavy legs of the Oceaner guard.

The new light alit off the back wall and reflected strangely upon the Raven. Her black feathers laced a bargello redolent of the Music's heart. A liniment for liturgy. Like two lovers lost in the lucid litany of the meadow's melody. The light found her form complete. Nothing was impartial. The light spiraled a strange way and seemed to be eating itself, but then it broke when the guard stepped in, fully.

"The sale is done," he said with eyes unsure and untested against the true blackness of Long-Arm's cell. Squinting, he said, "You may go, but don't go far."

The man's heavy boots pivoted, and he stepped beyond the small opening. Long-Arm stammered for a moment. He was unsure how long he had been locked within the enclosure. He was tired from his waking dreams, the oak's face, the Raven rising.

In time, not much but some, he stood up and ambled through the door and found what was left of their village: blackness and silvery smoke wafting in a seemingly endless wave of wind. Every tent, every tree, even the great Star Oak, was crushed obsidian.

All had burned and a great fire had burned all.

The sky was a dull crimson, and it was impossible to tell the time of day or the season for that matter. The crimson was paling into pink atop plants, which were spikey and snapped at his heels defensively like turtles. They were a dark and muddy green and looked as though they were preparing for something. Some continual flame. Some war that was already clashing.

The Glei was dry, its once green-brown riverbed paling in drought. The yellow stench of sulfur rose as rotting fish and colored the air. Flies, many and also one, waved in a great biting flutter, a putrid breath.

The stream had been diverted at its headwaters to the Oceaners' camp beyond the village. The enslaved Waters had skipped their banks to water their aqueous life. The Glei, the once animate stream. No more.

The Oceaners' imperial camp was fortified by rath and great earthworks and lay a mile beyond the village. Innumerable and tall tents waned beneath the shadow of the Mountain and obscured the view of any scouts. Tents stretched across the horizon and were consumed, minute by minute, by the reaching arm of the Rim's shadow.

Mathgen's bridge stood as an algae-encrusted and muscle-covered megalithic monument to some unknown god. To a god unknown.

All was mayhem, and her bedlam had become all.

Long-Arm walked alone across what was their village. His feet found nothing familiar. Beyond the shadow of the circling vultures and their fish flying in talons, he was alone. The Land was breathless, although the wind tore in gales hitherto foreign to the valley. Not a soul was in sight—Teyrnon and Pryderi never returned, the fire-blackened bones of the Old Mother stumbled shambolically to his left, the once-enduring rhythm of falling irons from the village's wrights and smiths, the pitter of pattering children, nothing remained. All was empty.

The spread valley and ancient forests that climb the rocky rises, the bald Mountain cutting the clouds, the fine carpet shag of falling mists that pour from moor and meadow alike, the sheer cliffs forgotten and cleft in the hills beyond, the effusive wells of Water bubbling at first and finding confluence when gravity finds its rhyme. This was the Land that walked in him.

But today was different. Twin fires vied for reflection in his wet eyes. The colors of the mid-day Sun paled into a singular dusking red and framed the silver mantle of clouds with obscurity. It was death without life. It was death without hope.

"It is too early to be dusk," he thought. "A grieving and strange light wafts reflection there and back again."

A smoke thundered from nowhere, with little warning, and the ashen ground below his feet fanned to envelop his figure until all he could see were curls and swirling greys that seemed to lift and litter his body up and upon the charred dirt. It cradled him, gently, like an orange rose that scuttles the ocean breeze over old tattered shutters. The air had the density of water.

Then, it rained. So much rain. Dense drops like rising mist fell from sparse clouds and glittered in pools of black. Everywhere, he could hear the sound of burning water, her dull roar, a gurgling cough of steam. Sodden Earth trodden in flame floated as detritus in the forming puddles, dismissing whatever looked in the shattered mirrors as an afterthought.

Life as postscript.

Life no more.

This was the Land that spoke.

Was.

This was no longer a living land.

Once, sure. But not today.

They were the Kinship of old.

They had their own names for it.

Names scraped in runes and woven by tongues long lost.

Tongues cut out may speak only little and speak only in wormy wiggles.

Like eels but dead and dying.

———————

The day was cresting into evening when Long-Arm fell upon Miach's scorched apothecary.

I don't know why his feet took him that way, but they did.
And I followed.

A millennium of mead that Cían was busy teaching Miach to make before he had left lay exposed and shattered on the stone floor.

"The Oceaners let themselves in. They always let themselves in," Long-Arm thought with blistering fingers that fumbled with the many glass shards.

He lifted one up, an amber glass bottle blown by a master. It was perfect, or at least reminded him of its once-attained perfection. A vessel, a boat of breath to heal and carry those who would carry it. But today, it was only a sliver of its once great hull, its ballast soaking back into Earth, drip over drip.

It was the largest shard strewn about that yet held on to the flower's medicine. He smelled it, the meager and shivering sliver of mead. He tasted the cross-pollination that Cían always told him and Miach about when the bee's buzz lifted the nectar's fizzing fuzz to create gold.

"Alchemy is real," Cían used to joke. "When it rains, silver becomes gold when the flaxenhaired fairyland unfolds."

"I thought the alchemists turn lead into gold?" Miach would ask, prodding his father along, always after a few draughts, tests that is, of their product.

"That is right! But what is lead but falling rain?" Cían would incant with his eyes pitted on theirs, his gentle smile smirking across ageless cheeks. "What is alchemy but those who understand that transformation is not change but becoming who you already are?"

"Becoming who you already are," Long-Arm thought as he sifted through broken memories, through a broken life, through ash.

Visions of their world visited him amongst the char and broken amber glass, but they never manifested around him, fully. Ancient conversations arose from the scorched Earth, but they didn't grow legs and walk with him. He was alone, but he wasn't lonely.

Jars of potent medicines were strewn about. A fire yet smoldering lay beyond. It held a visage of dried herbs, the strangely inviting aroma wafting gently from the embers. A breeze followed the rain that tousled the rising and dawdling herbs, guiding the last fibers up into the invisible chimney of stacked stone.

Stones that pled for mercy. Stones plying with grace. Stones that spoke in runes of Mountains past, when rivers and glacial ice tore and scaped their valley into being.

Today, blinding beads of boiling blood fell as rain that crackled a maroon mottle upon the stones. He looked up. Swallows wheeled and jousted beneath the brilliant breath-swept sky.

"Was it their blood that was falling? Or their tears?" he thought.

Beyond the ash, life, or what was left of her, rose in an acrid heap that ruddered the dim vaults above into something beautiful. The Sun burnished a red silhouette, flaring emissions of radiation that fell upon this world as droplets of boiling blood.

"It's not the swallow. The Sun is crying!"

A token blight, the red Sun's tears, of omens past when their fathers waged war against the Oceaners and lost. They escaped by sailing to the northern isles of this world, beyond the Rim. The Old Ones lived and learned the ancient Arts and returned, in time, with powers and furrowed features like fairies, blonde by the burnt belly of the Sun.

The persistent beauty worked to remind him of the river Cailleach's spring garlic and his brother's insistent medicine.

"Roots are not tethers but tendrils for exploration," Miach's words floated about him like petals loosed in the wind or herbs sailing like stones in the smoke.

But he couldn't stay long in this place and so he said a simple goodbye and walked on. The young oak astride the tent was chopped at the base. Its leaves curdled like spoiled milk.

But it was not burnt.

———————

Over the wind and ash, falling rain and blood, a drumming rose.

A wood stick beating rapt skin.

A chiseled tree thrashing oiled leather.

Its rhythm rhymed and then resonated with the pounding rain

around him, but it was warm. A thrumming wave thrusting through dark spaces. Striking and shivering the middle of his chest. But off center to the left, his left.

Bone-snap beating into his chest like dawning light—immediately but without either haste or hesitancy. It was a sparkling star swirling the day awake.

The deep drumming called him on and awoke him from the memory of Miach and their lost world like a lightning snap. The swallows disappeared and the rain stopped, its blood curdling at his feet like curled fingers.

A few hundred paces beyond the tents where the Plant clan once lived, an alien color fought against the ashen landscape and flitted behind a crumbing stone wall. A coral-colored twist, a pink and red tassel that choked two bare ankles.

He walked cautiously on and ambled toward the stone but hesitated as he neared. The last life he saw was the Oceaner guard that let him out of his cell. And so, he approached with caution.

The Land about him spoke of a great devastation. It was still warm, life yet crumbling into ash. "But where are The People?" his heart questioned.

A dank silence echoed without harmony over what was left of the village, but a moldy smell wafted back, like hay after a storm. A life that was dead but not digested.

"Do you remember the old trees that drank the blood of sleeping heroes?" a gentle voice asked as it fluttered from behind the falling wall in front of him.

The voice was familiar. Memories rising in its cadence. Long-Arm walked forward, faster. Trying to set his eyes upon the voice, to know what his ears already understood.

"—Of those silly enough to slumber against their sharp roots?" said the coral voice, but this time it echoed against his back.

She was behind him.

He snapped around head first like a horse on a fly and turned to behold a young girl standing within arm's reach.

Her deep blue and strangely browless eyes looked straight into his, and they seemed to pull him forward. A shiver rose from his spine and colored the hairs on his back. He tried to look away. Tried. But he couldn't.

"They are for those who need them," she said, kindly.

"What are?" he returned without meaning to.

"Names," the girl said simply and with a graceful kindness hitherto foreign within the landscape—her smile seemed to alight the black Earth into orange flame once again.

"Names are beacons that bring the heavens down to walk with us," he returned, the familiar taste of this conversation welling into his throat like bile.

At this, she released his eyes with a subtle sweep of her finger. His attention then fell to the coral-colored buckskin pants that were too short for her long legs and showed her shins. The pants were rugged but not rigid. He looked at her feet, and surprise overtook him.

Her metatarsal bones lingered up past her ankles like the elongated greenwood of spring oak branches and extended into her shins. She stood like a horse.

His eyes then trailed up her legs, and, landing at her waist, he could just make out a flit of feathers or feather-like hairs that filtered the red light of the falling Sun into reflections of simple blacks and sheened forests of greens.

"Names are not for those who wear them, or hold them, or live in them," she said, breaking his trance.

He looked up, fully this time, and connected with the strange girl. He looked at her. She looked at him. Two eyes meeting each other.

"Who are you?" he asked. A strength settled in his words.

"My name is Bacharigu, the youngest of The Mothers," she responded in welcomed simplicity.

"I am Long-Arm."

"I know, we've met."

"Under the oak, I remember. And when the Old Mother—"

"Then why did you—"

"It is polite, no?" he said, smiling the color yellow.

She smiled back, and they held each other's gaze for a moment. The rain sprinkled about them, between them, but something was different like slumbering heroes rising from roots or blood waving through parched veins once again.

"It was all so very different back then. When we ran together and climbed the Mountain for mugwort," she said.

"We?" Long-Arm leaned forward unnaturally.

"When we ambled through oak and willow," Bacharigu said, ignoring his question, "and before Breoch, the beautiful and shapely, split us apart in arrogance. Chaining us from each other, they stripped us of ourselves. But, in doing so," she continued, "they brought about flowers that grow upon stone and rising ashes that surge under splashing blood into heroes anew."

"I watched the Old Mother burn," Long-Arm said, a shiver welling into a tear.

"You watched them burn water," the girl returned.

"What is the difference?"

"Steam falls after it collects, and condensation is a world-shaping force," Bacharigu returned, nearly snarling.

A strange energy flirted between them. It seemed to unite her words with Earth under his unshod feet and surged up his own body like a charge of horses, of feet falling a chaotic syncopation, an entropic expansion of dust rising into a tornado so complete that it created what it destroyed.

"Your name is *Lámfada*, you say?" she asked.

The tornado of dust sparkling like spears in the strange light cast from her eyes.

"Yes, Long-Arm," the boy returned.

"No, today she calls you Sammil, the many-joined, the harpist, poet, and bard, wielding not a quill but a spear."

He stammered back. A great cloud lingered above them. The Old Mother's condensation finally collecting into a torrent. Fanning a falling flame that shadowed a thundering bolt. The world shook and cleft a chasm.

"Awake!" the girl screamed, stepping forward, her eyes piercing his chest like drums. The world shook again. A thrumming arose from the new cavern so deep that it seemed to shatter the bones of stones. Bacharigu inhaled a pregnancy of wind, a distention of grace, and the landscape was sucked inside of her like a waterfall of light.

Then, she continued, "Undertake the battle before you. Awake! Slumber not upon roots but erect an edifice. Undertake the hard slaughter, the rising steam falling upon you, smiting bodies, boiling blood, like fallen stars and gods rising from mounds. You met the *Máithrín*, yes. Your axe and biting steel found her deep ochre heartwood. But you did not fell her as you think. For long has the omens foretold when biting steel would erect a dolmen in the heartwood of stone, a place of passage for our people, a new pillar upon the plain! A pillar of peace.

"They ushered you to commence their undoing. They commanded you to untie their hold. Arise! Awake from the grange anew, the light is upon you! Cleanse the Land, she cries out, she begs you: Arise! Awake!"

At this, the girl fell over, overcome by some internal torrent that swelled into completion. She fell head first like a tumbling statue into the chasm created by her words. She fell into the Land's boiling heart. And then, all was still.

Long-Arm, the boy now called Sammil, blinked and looked down. He saw only silence.

A sea of words floated about in crashing but hushed waves like dragonflies. Then, a Raven shot up from the deep and knocked him back. The chasm closed shut before he could regain sight. Stumbling to his feet, the black dirt at his hands transformed into something hard and something new. A spear. But he knew it well, the great *Sleá* that used to rest above the hearth of the long house—its javelin-like shaft with tipped iron reflecting the winter fire into the hall and lighting the space with great silvery light.

In that moment, it reflected only the light of the girl's words as their symbols silently drifted about as hushed white ghosts.

The strangely familiar grooves of battles past that etch and travel the length of the weapon felt warm to him like he had been holding this spear his entire life. His hands knew it, and it knew his hands.

Looking up, Sammil caught the path of the Raven. She was flying to the long house atop the hill, a subtle plume of smoke rising under the red of the dusking Sun. Silhouettes of life beat deep shadows through the open windows.

Everyone that remained had gathered in the long house. They waited and were waiting.

He knew what he had to do.

He knew what he was called to be.

That evening, only moments later,
in the long house.

The fire, now moved into the middle of the hall, was high and bright.

It shot stars into the ceiling that appeared to float up beyond the glittering night sky like fireflies migrating home. The flame thrust ochre light and shadows upon the solemn columns of The People sitting against the wall.

Architecture may be scribed lines over Earth to vault the wind and divert our eyes to the holy, but in this moment, the oak-hewn house's spirit descended to draw The People down, to look upon the wattle-and-daub that capped the night away and cupped the silvery Water of the Moon in grey-bark slabs of yet living oak.

The fire was let to die as the room darkened to a pulse. The long house fell into a deep silence as the last flame flickered above the wood with a twist and a curl and then lapped against the deep hall's final breath.

After a long black moment, a rattle shook the night awake. A drum followed, then many more. Masked figures of woodland creatures danced their draggled limbs. Their feet stomping with the drums and fingers playing, like sorcerers, under the rattles' shake and twist. The music picked up, and the dancers followed. A hallucinogenic haze lifted The People up, and they were each carried in their own ways by the music.

Some twisted.

Others stomped.

Still, a few slithered like standing snakes.

The transient edges of the rhythm popped like embers, and the circling mass glided and lunged aggressively in the dim dank air under the wholly world-like architecture of the reliquary, the hall.

Bacharigu, now at once a girl, spun in place with arms fully feathered and extending beyond her. Ogham, he who was their language, twirled with spiraling fingers that curled like runes the long cloth that streamed below his ankles, a slashing wave of color in the otherwise colorless night.

The music then rose and broke free from the dancers. It walked across the benches where the herbalists used to work and wafted the loose and forlorn herbs into a hurricane, a rolling tsunami, of healing.

After a while, hours or minutes it was unknown, the music and the dancers began to settle when the last red-orange embers of the fire crackled into a cold smoke, and all came to rest like liquid once stirred but now coming into final repose.

At this, the boy once called Long-Arm strode silently, more shaman than priest, to the front of the long house. Miach's flowers waved in the lingering smoke to his left. Bacharigu's winged dance flirted with the darkness in the corner of the hall. Standing straight and sure, now confident in his power, Sammil spoke in a sure voice that was sheltered in a whisper. A life cloaked in the night.

"Harmonizes Us to All Things used to stand here as I do now," he said to the weavers and the poets, the carpenters and sorcerers. "In but a matter of days, we will be forced to convene under Breoch once again. What evils will he ask upon us? Miach may have separated his arm from his body, but he has many plans."

The boy's heart was hammering, his blood thick and growing more so. The feeling of iron eating wood pulsed through his veins like the cadenced swing of an axe. The great tree's words etched upon his limbs like sweat that streaks under the summer Sun, but worse, but living.

Sammil continued, "The Harp, our Harp, the daughter of the *Máithrín*, the creator of all things and the life that dwells in the pulse of all creation, once dwelled and lived with us. Her music carried us," he said, floating his fingers in the air above his head. "Her music was everything and in everything was her music."

A chorus smiled a loving laughter as the music's memory floated from person to person. It skipped like the dancing frost of the late winter morning and twirled in glittering golds like the bouncing snowflakes that always follow. Tears then fell and a cry was heard. Soon, the darkness settled and the fire's embers popped.

Sammil continued, repeating the words of the *Máithrín*, "When the music sought harmony, she gave us the Harp. When the plain sought life, she gave us the Mountain's pillars. And when that life journeyed for a container, she gave us this reliquary," he said holding his hands out signifying the long house. "—and she gave us this representation of our world," he said as he lifted The Mother's Caldron up from the shadows at his feet.

At this, Bacharigu walked forward and stood next to him. She was now dressed in red and looked older than he remembered.

"The music creates, the pillars live, and the great reliquary reminds us of rebirth. It gives us a metabolism for metamorphosis," she said.

"The *Máithrín* has instructed me," Sammil added, his eyes connecting with Bacharigu's and his gaze searching her face as he spoke, "to spin three circles upon each other. That we would live in this circle, with her, and in this circle, her life would live."

Then, holding the Caldron, he took an iron rod from the fire and etched the *Máithrín's* symbol into its face, like three snakes eating each other and then, finally, becoming one as they came together.

"The symbol finding her perfection," he said, "when we find ourselves in the heart of the spiral. One line forming three complete and twisting units. One becoming three. Three becoming one." His gaze scythed over the dark hall and landed, finally, on Bacharigu. He looked into her eyes, speaking directly to her, and incanted, "The Kinship, Oneness, and harmony finding one another in the music living in the center of the spiral."

You call this symbol a triskelion—an ancient motif that consists of three curved segments that radiate from a central core or point.

But it did not call itself that.

This is the danger of the modern heart—it lacks the words because it lacks the harmony. Memory is nowhere.

Triskelion comes from the Greek word tri— for three and –skelos for legs, or Three Legs. It was named by the conquerors of this ancient and gathering people. It was named so that they had power over it, like Breoch said as the Old Mother burned.

How very modern of you that, to see the life in this symbol, you must give it legs—not appendages like plants or limbs like trees. No, legs like you.

What did it call itself?

That is a fine question.

Why don't you ask?

"This is what she gave to us," Sammil continued, still holding the Caldron for all to see.

An aroma of burnt clay rose into the rafters, and a yellow-ochre color fell in response—the oak-hewn blades and beams cried when they saw the sign and cast their dust down.

At this, Bacharigu asked, "How long since the *Fáil* stone screamed its acceptance of us, our right to occupy and have Kinship with this Land, as this Land, an honor rotating around our singular heart's symphony with her sympathetic threads woven in weft and warp, brocaded in sinews of blood and bone, a harmony seeking resonance when our Kinship finds its Oneness?" Again, her belly now swelling like she ate the world to find the words.

The sound of distant thunder rolled through the now cloudless night. A new Moon. Complete darkness. The thunder was far enough afield that it ached the hills a slumber their spirit did steal, and yet close enough, still, to scare the animals into their burrows. The room shuddered but held still. Life was listening.

Smiling, the boy returned, "Yes, in the age before the Moon lit the dim of the world and kissed the Waters in the wakeless nights, our fathers fought the Oceaners and lost. This is true. Our kin fought against kings for occupancy, not over the Land, but ourselves—the ability to alone decide our fate but never to become lonely in that lot.

"Today and also all days since that fateful day," Sammil continued, "the Oceaners and their boy-king have sought to separate us. It is clear to me. It has been made clear to me like the clearest of clear river Waters: we must find peace. We must fight once again, but not for a portion of the Land like our fathers did. No! We must rise as the Land, with the Land, in the Land."

Sammil's words were strong, but all did not agree. The carpenter, one of the oldest of the village, stood and challenged the boy. "Mark me," he said, "as the days wane into winter, the hare will scurry through their hearts and the stag through their bellies. They cannot live like we do, surviving from the sustenance of the mare's blood, and they will want. We should wait and draw them out."

Others agreed and lifted their support. Everyone muttered to their neighbors, dialoguing and conversing about strategy and the strain of the decision.

Then, the carpenter continued, "Their penchant for feud and internecine strife is our greatest bulwark, our finest defense. Their compulsion to deconstruct, their impulse to destroy, will first destroy them, I think."

More of the Síraide shifted in the darkness and admitted approval. The carpenter's weight was winning, his logic tipping the scales.

"Besides," the carpenter continued, strengthened by the support, "what is the point? They have done their worst, and we have grown gills amongst them. So what if our knives rust without the love of lard? So what if our tables rot without laughter? What if the plain becomes a pond? We have our lives. You saw what they did to Miach, to the Old Mother."

Then, Gamal, the doorkeeper of the long house, who has otherwise been silent in this tale, joined and probed the darkness, "What hope do we have against their forces? What Art do you carry to save us from Balor and his boy-king?"

Sammil looked down and away from The People. He cherished the darkness for what it was—a silent peace ready for fire and its flame.

After a while, he returned, "We lost, that is correct. Your memories are alive. My friends," he continued, now looking up and into their eyes, "this is not a war, but a moment for alchemy. From rain to mead, lead to gold, today we become what we already are—the Land. If she is not free, how can we be? If she is not alive, how can we live?"

A despondent cry uncoiled from his throat that choked into a stammering hiss deep into his chest. The first fire fell from his lips, like the mare, like Pryderi. Clenched teeth, lungs gasping for air, mind mounting into memory, the boy sat down, unaware that he carried this Art. At this, the air amongst them lulled as the music swelled, rising from the fire that now burst from its lone embers, boiling them in a mist.

Standing up, the boy then said, "The plain is our hearth, the pillars are our womb, and this Caldron is now our strength. The battle is not war but transformation. The fight is not against our foes but for ourselves. This is the alchemy. But it must be our decision. *Fódla*, the Land, is waiting. The Land, our blood.

"Tomorrow, the Sun will bathe us in glittering morning gold," he continued, now with arms raised and towering above him. "Tomorrow and every day after and before, we will harmonize with all things. Life lives to mark us, surely. I understand the world of your words. But we must sing fearlessly, not courageously. For she asks for harmony cast without fear. It is true: at times, we find more force in memory, the aftermath of battle, than the moments that we walked upon the field. These are the marks that rankle and chafe as they become memory and so remain peers to our bleeding and beating hearts forever."

The eastern Sun now dawned the first pink and red rays through the window overlooking the garden. The great Ash tree a black and burnt silhouette against it all.

"To find peace, we must find ourselves *within* the music. A worldview is seeing the notes. A worldsense is becoming the music herself," Sammil said simply. "If we do not fight, we will forever live asunder. The battle is not about defeating our enemy but finding ourselves upon the plain of pillars."

At this, he shifted his weight and stepped fully into his place in the circle. The fire roared in the middle and reflected red light against The People's pale faces.

"What Art do you practice?" questioned Gamal's voice in the rising light.

"Question me," the boy returned, "I am Sammil, the many-joined, the Artist that Pryderi brought forth to erect a symbol, a resonance echoing from the heart of harmony, the *Máithrín*, metamorphizing the wonders into the wonderful. I fell from the yellowing mane of the Horse. Today, this morning, we ride. Today, this morning, we will find peace."

At this, everyone, even the carpenter, nodded their heads to the rhythm of his words.

The Sun, now golden, rose to meet them.

Later that morning, upon the plain.

A hurricane of Horses stomped impatiently.
Water gurgled as it splashed under their many feet. It did not slow them down. It could not slow down their torrent, their rising ferocity.

The Sun slowly gathered the plain in his boiling clasp. The plain readied for the letting. The dew burned into a putrid vapor and a subtle silvery mist fluttered amongst the grasses that were waving dryly on the islands of high ground. Grasses now fully soused under the coming torrent and rasped against the Horses' many hooves.

The air smelled of rising Earth.

The Earth was colored by the falling breath of battle.

I circled overhead, waiting for the mayhem.

Sammil readied the ranks for the coming chaos.

The pilgrimage was finished.

The worship brayed to begin.

A thousand thousand feet beat as one as the Síraide's horns roared their scabbards empty, and the din of pounding Earth clamored forward in raw red screams.

The battle began.

This was not a Bronze Age pitched battle as you may expect. There were no tactics, no strategies written on maps under canvas white tents by generals and professional warriors.

This was not a battle led by those in the rear.

No.

This was a tornado—the Land rising to decolonize your straight lines, to destroy your fake architecture, your heavenly lit clearstories. A chaotic castration of naves from your phallic apses, vicars screaming as they were dragged by their hair into the streets and stoned.

It screamed a madness from its very heart and it led with its heart in its hands.

It was a wind rising to create our world once again in the image of ourselves—the all of us—not you.

Screams echoed as swords glittered a muted reflecting red that dripped a putrid ochre light dribbling down the tangled blood of locked limbs from blunted edges to hilt.

Sammil stumbled as he struggled to make sense of the confusion around him. He leaped over the littered plain with the Horse clan and pushed forward.

The Robin clan fell in a pitched battle on his right but worked on routing their foes with the river at their backs—its clearest of clear Waters now flowing red with corpses. Islands of bubbling bodies and bowels.

The Plant clan loomed large in fibrous phalanxes that twisted and pulled against the feet of their foes, ripping limb from body in plump plops of synovial fluids.

Sammil lunged into the mayhem of a pitched scene and thrust his spear into the throat of an Oceaner, and turning, he sliced the bowels of another, who then fumbled with his loosed stomach's nearly infinite intestines as though he cradled water in his palms.

Bacharigu, now half crow and half Mother, rode a white Horse and swung feverishly, cutting down those around her. She hacked through shields and broke the arms underneath, ulnas cracking and humerus marrow exploding like shrapnel. Her Horse was cut from under her and, now fully flying in the momentum, she landed the blunt end of her spear in the flattened face of her foe.

Twisting like some whirlybird of death, she struck two foes at once, one falling back, shrieking yellow screams as he slapped worthlessly at the blood that spew from his groin. It rushed like spring Mountain Water. But red.

She fought with an enflamed heartache and her force crushed bone and limb and pounded until plumes of blood fumed around her.

Slithering and still shaking sea monsters were strewn about the plain and were hacked to death by a havoc packed so tight that the Land's litter seemed stamped together by nails.

Harsh was the thunder that struck the battle, the shouting of warriors and the clashing of shields. The rattling of emptying quivers, the sound and winging of arrows and javelins. The clash of metal against something more real, more singular, made not in heat but in the hearts of all—almost musical.

The plain became a river of blood and many Oceaners fell from their upright war postures and beat their heads together as they sat. The hopeless beating against hopelessness.

This is something masters do not often anticipate.
The ferocity of love.

Mathgen, the sorcerer, called upon the Land and the stones rose and shuttled as he cast the Mountain upon the valley and rolled its great summit down, flattening those who sought to flatten.

Firgol mac Mamois, the memory-carrier, showered three fires of falling flames upon the heads of the Oceaners and the spewing magma cleaned their façades from their faces.

Then, the Cupbearer caused the lakes of the Land and their valley moors to dry up and the Oceaners stumbled in drought, cut down in a waterless torpor.

The eternal ones, The People of Síraide, struck their master's head against the cliffs, like a hand in a serpents nest, their furry was like a face up to fire. A thousand thousand flags whipped the wind straight. Flags painted with prayers. Prayers painted by their peoples. Peoples carried by their music.

"Fight! Oh, slaughterous battle!" Sammil cried, his words becoming a white Horse that galloped across the plain with a red hand slapped upon its flanks. "There is cutting and contending forces, the phantoms, men of the Land, beware!

"Align to truth without choice, following furies! Burst forth, overthrowing, dividing, the black truth: little white death ring, Hale! Woe! Sinister and fierce! A sanctified omen after cloud shadows our victory will spread! A deadly brilliance, the Sun rises!"

His speech, words between warding blows, caused a great surge over the Land, like an earthquake welling up from heaven to Earth.

When one of The People fell, The Children of Cécht sank their maimed body into The Mother's Caldron, which now bore the *Máithrín's* symbol, and they would emerge whole again and return to the battle.

Then, at the height of the furry, when all came to a point, Sammil found Balor. Attendants worked to open the king's eye with a polished handle that passed through its lid. It had poisonous power and many of the Síraide lay still at his feet. Robin and Horse, Stag also, were littered about, and the death threatened a collapse.

"In the end," Sammil said, circling Balor, his eyes impervious to the poison, "though I am a small boy who is striking, this is your day of death."

"Lift up mine eyelid further, lad," Balor croaked, shifting his steel from one hand to the other. A fresh grip. "Lift mine eye that I may see the babbler who is conversing with me."

"Flowing seas grind people together. The seas destroy flesh. But you walk on Land," Sammil said.

"I walk upon *my* Land," Balor returned.

At this, Balor peered at the white willows and ash that lay beyond the plain and they toppled into crashing tumbles. The trees lay prostrate against the quaking Earth and left craters of overturned roots and circular tangles of shallow ponds—life hanging onto humus and Water filling the void.

"No, you monster of little waves, you magician of little worlds," Sammil returned. "You may no longer take nuts or milk. Unripe grain or grain at all. You may not take honor's price of honor itself. The trees may fall but you cannot cast death's final blow. Defeat is shame on the shoulders of a god. From our roots life springs yet! But today is your day of death, for your roots are already rotting."

The two warriors circled each other as the miasma of the plain welled around them in crashing waves. But all was silent—the circle traced by their feet became a sanctuary for silence, for the boy's life.

At last, Sammil, the boy, the son of mare and mugwort, the brother of Miach, an Artist at his work, leapt forward with the *Sled's* tipped iron reflecting the light of the rising Moon.

. . .

"Dad, can we skip to the part where they get the Harp back, you know——" the boy asked, pivoting in his bed and checking on his bedroom's nightlight, "——by becoming *visible?*"

"No, my son. It is late," his father said with a short laugh.

"Tomorrow?"

"Yes, tomorrow. But now, it is time to rest. We have all the time in the world——" his father returned, patting his red haired head and placing the ancient peeling leather book gently upon the nightstand.

"——And no time at all," the boy returned, finishing his father's sentence with a smirk.

The boy closed his eyes, gently, and wrapped his long arms around a stuffed animal cresting his elbow like the Sun below the Mountain——a roan horse with a yellowing mane.

"Dad?"

"Yes, son?"

Then darkness. The lights switched off. His father turned around in the doorway, his hand working its frame like a wright and a carpenter.

"What does it mean to find peace?"

"What do you think?" he returned without moving.

"I try not to think," the boy returned, smiling and coughing weakly into a gentle laugh.

"Maybe you're right," his father said, and then again, "Maybe you are right."

"Does Pryderi ever return?"

"That is another story for another day, don't you think?"

"Dad," the boy retorted with childlike emphasis, making the middle letter its own syllable. "I try not to think!"

A smile crested a subtle wave in the dark.

"Good night, Lu," His father said.

"Good night, Dad," the boy returned, already drifting into sleep.

At this, his father closed the door and walked silently down the hall. He flipped on the TV, as was his habit since she had left, but at least he had given up smoking. He watched the drone footage——caped by letters in banners of blue and red that waved below the screen—of bombs igniting flashes of horrendous light, bodies like distended bowls exploding into the air, children screaming and rocking desolately on devastated desert curbs, and young protesters with blue flags clouding over university campuses with Gucci purses draped like tribal tapestries.

Click. He changed the channel. Money machines screamed and rolled as a perfectly diverse arrangement of newscasters debated inflation and the next presidential election.

Click. He changed the channel. A press conference. State governments have joined together to sue a pharmaceutical company for wrongly advertising their products as life-saving when, in fact, it only saved the lives of some but killed many others. Nothing was mentioned about their other products that destroy life in the billions. Children mostly.

Click. He changed the channel, overwhelmed and drifting to sleep himself. A drone video of a hardwood forest that once draped over the ancient Mountains of Appalachia is being clear-cut, then sprayed with herbicides, then planted in pine for pulp. The local paper is there, and the mayor of the small city as well, dressed in business casual and wearing blue jeans with the tags still on. The camera continues panning up to a lone bird on a limb above the men speaking. The town is offering a sustainability award, it seems, to the logging crew—a sustainable business that planted one hundred thousand trees this year. A record.

He looked back to Lu's room, the light snaking down the hall and under his door. The strange and agile blue energy of the TV set flickered. A tear welled and fell. It scudded over his scrubby cheeks and danced around the deep rusting red scar that arched from his chin to his cheekbone. It was salty.

A wing flit a fine black against the empty hall.

"A wing?" he thought, unsure if he was dreaming or still awake.

And that's when it happened. The world cleft like in the storybook and only fractals remained. The world within becoming the world without—the wing, the trickster, the fractaler. The Lord of the in-between. She lives not at the hearth, the marble halls of justice, the monastery or the Montessori.

She lives in the silence—the symbols in the dark.

Symbols of the dusking dawn, the dark and star-lit night, those lights of the long dead, those whose light carries memory and nothing else. Maybe love.

Yes, Love.

The boundary.

The boundary walker.

The thin veil between Heaven and Earth.

Told on wings of dark black feathers.

"What does it mean to find peace?" the child Lu's voice flickered through the darkness and into the father's heart-mind. It bled in his chest. He looked down the hall.

Here ends the first rib-bone of The Rimwalker Series.

Go raibh míle maith agat.
táim thar a bheith buíoch díot.
do chara, ffrith.

PRELUDE

A HISTORY OF THE CATACLYSM

YEAR 2049
HAMLET NO. 5.2, LANES 11-12

When the rubble settles, those cursed with living will talk about the great Cataclysm. Horrors cloaked in hushed tales riding the dimly lit corners of whispers. They will tell of the final moment, a moment when a smile ticked the end of the world.

Tomes will be written about the destruction. Some will take on an academic provenance, contributing to a field of abstract study, satisfying an orbit radiating from cerebral groins. Others, probably the anthropologists, will pen power dynamics by dissecting the cause with trowels, layer by layer, object by object, coming to their own conclusions.

It will also tell its own story...

Those living will walk in words that stumble over the fell, foul bones of blackened cities and the charred trunks of trees. The Survivors will fade into the walled Hamlets. One by one, they will be rounded up like livestock and herded into prisons of madness, those stuffed up bowels, those swelling corpses, those Hamlets with their gates shut, barred. All becoming slaves to Salience. Chained to a prominence.

Great alien armies will debate its causes. Entire leagues will thrust through the cosmos in search for new lands, new Earths. New science walking on the backs of its failed colleagues.

Failing still.

Though they who live will mourn their lives, no one, not even the strangely suckled offspring, will understand what really happened.

No one will remember.

This is the Cataclysm.

No one will remember.

For it all began with a thought.

I

lukot-segno di blâwo gaisseto

THE MOUSETRAP OF YELLOWING MANE

YEAR UNKNOWN
THE RIM

It was a luxury to burn. It was his final affluence. He was alone in the din of the winter woods and he was screaming and he was running and he was naked.

His first thought was that he was falling. Comes up alert, blood rushing to unbalance him so that he nearly tipped over, just slightly, that lurching feeling winning in his gut, the sense of free falling. Strange memories of cliffs cascading stone by stone into a broad river flit before his eyes like a sheath of flame. He looked down, not knowing what to expect—

But what he saw changed everything: he was not falling and there were no cliffs roiling rocks into rivers, just his legs running. Running? Running! yes, so much like falling.

But the billowing column of fire was real. Lashed his naked back, is teeth ripping into the soft flesh that laces ribs like spiderwebs, hunting for the dripping bubbles below. Tearing like jealous lions.

The man *was* burning alive.

He sent his fingers around to feel the throbbing pain on his back and dug them in through the cracks in his skin—skin stretched so thin where his heart is trying to spill out of the back, through the ribs— touching the webby whiteness in there, that stringy tissue, making him gag so fast, the feeling coming from somewhere else. It's more like a tightness groaning a line between his back and his legs, a sudden bulge, a burst disc, just above his hip.

The flames, eerie and strange, pulled heavily, rending his body in two, milling it with a dull cleaver, spitting his blood like sawdust. The flames a blind butcher working the woodmill. The flames a savvy sawyer cutting meat. That was why he was screaming: it hurt.

But why he was running was a different story...

Fight me, he could've demanded. Striking his chest with balled fists ready to brawl. He wouldn't. He couldn't. Is running, is light on the balls of his feet, to save this, to—

But he had no energy left. No beat to his blood to rally the drama, the effort. No fire in his body, not anymore, not after—

The fire licking with flames, fully now and sharp. Taking all time with it. And bright. An unfamiliar bliss rose as unseen swells in his chest with every lapping lick of the flames, and he smiled when he thought about things being eaten, of things changing and being changed.

Like actually.

His eyes saw very little. But he *smelled* everything.

The smoke curling into a thready soot and whirling now in waving rips. Spiraling into itself. It was strong and thick. Intertwisting stitches of grey lace rising outward like a blast, a firebomb purling over a flat plain. Drowning him in its aromatic seasoning. Like his old life was just an incaustious spice to be splattered upon the hot cooking stone of his new.

The burning man's mind suckled on the many white globs of

thought. Body melting, releasing a certain steam. It was only then that his memories swam like Salmon: spinal fluids becoming a river, his mind, a deep liquid lake. He felt their fins flutter as shivers rose to the surface, dotting his naked skin, skin now stretched thin over his jagged spine with many blisters and bubbles and hanging flesh.

He heard their Salmon-y song, their reticent rhythm about remembrance and all that, and he attended to his own carcass falling apart—not with pops or craggy rips, but with sluicy slides of melting meat.

Such it is when burning alive.

It hurts, yeah.

That is why he was screaming.

But he was also running...

2

ON SALIENCE

YEAR 2049

HAMLET NO. 5.2, LANES 11-12

It was an age of experts. It was their season. Upon the urgency of the end, they were looked to like bleating lambs in search of teats.

The specialists were the source. They had names for the Cataclysm that walked over ruins and mass graves like sliver ash in the winter wind. They had names, but they never shared them. The specialists lost life like a child loses rocks when the school bell rings, storied stones splashing back into gravel at the beckon of intellect, letting the experience of meaning become outweighed by the purpose of it.

The specialist was not the reason the Cataclysm happened, but most thought that they were related. Even distantly...

Experts sought a narrow field like the Roman blood-rattle of Cannae, placing the weak in the middle, knowing that conscience makes cowardice and that conscience and its cowardice only break when pushed. They sought narrow fields, for narrow fields are achievable ones—conquerable ones, commandable ones. And conquering is only a potentiality of human experience because of the specialist.

It is their thing, if you will.

It was what they are good at, like rocks for gravel.

For generalists care not to conquer fields. No, they yearn to play in them, to run in them, to dance in them. To sing.

The Salience and its Dome went by different names in different blocs. In the Hamlets, especially in Hamlet no. 5.2, it was just the Dome and Salience. As it was what the Cataclysm's government and its red-furred homeofficer's elected, the corners rounded off, nothing garish or gaudy to purchase. Ostentation was a luxury of the dead, the damned. It carried little tender among the living, the Survivors, those in specie to the Hamlets. The poor staying poor and their words with them. Their worlds too. Chained in rust. Locked behind broad, concrete walls. Language given from the top.

In the City, bustling and bright, the risks were greater, but so were the rewards. The City of Central, the faithful, the pious. They lived like nothing happened. Tinsel upon the plain, lily white, and celibate—and terrible for it. The City's faithful grown so fat and thick that all satellites led into them like streams of sustenance. No hinterlands or outliers. Just the smell of blood, yeah.

The City's sacred chaplets and their blooming alters of blood rising like sap. The religious fanatics of The Holontology could sting and divert, and they suckled to sprout legs in their new world, the world following the end, the world they had certain names for but never shared. For structures abhor source, they make mapping a maze, good medicine an appanage. And the more one tried to understand the architecture of their mastery, the more one was colonized by it. And confused.

Such the Hamlets came into being, as they are now, on Day One after the Cataclysm. Such our story lives in Hamlet no 5.2, somewhere between Lanes 11 and 12.

But names aren't the only variable to be calculated. The only nuance to give pause, or power. Color was a second, and color was abatable. Not inexorable. It was living and thus worthy of dying. It was living, unlike everything else. Everyone else beyond the preternatural creatures well camouflaged like stonefish expressed as little flowers or blades of cutting mist that transformed whoever attempted to leave the refuge, the walled Hamlet, to raise their head above the walls, to see something else, into a bloody mess of tattered flags. And skin.

Sped forward into futures, color had power over time and space, some even saw color as the fourth dimension, the dimension beyond the possible, beyond the fakery of this modern man, and so there was no cause of conservancy following the Cataclysm, Salience and their City said, when the future was just another name for the past. The past but compoundingly more dreadful.

This is what Salience said. This is who Salience was.

But something told *him* something else. That they were wrong, so wrong, so really *very* fucking wrong...

3

AN ORCHESTRA
OF PIPES

YEAR 2049
HAMLET NO. 5.2, LANES 11-12

Lu woke in burning sweat.

The salt of his body seeping like cold, black oil. Slow and sluggish. Sweat puddling around him. The bed becoming a pond of fetid fluids. Broth burning new and lithe pathways, cutting new maps in the sheets for new monsters to follow. The cold water dripped down his back. He laid still on the bed and slowly shook his hands free from sleep. But he couldn't stall the remembering. The murk of nightmares steadily becoming a morass like cold piss in polyester sheets—

Fuck, he said in words or out of them.

That was his educated conclusion: he was fucked.

They were all fucked, royally fucked, the Survivors and their new world, any and all hope—fucked.

The continuum that produced untold strings of sleepless nights seared his skin's pores like hot iron rods. Burning shut, closing them in fusty and blistering scabs, branding his body with their strange symbols. Making him buoyant when he just wanted to drown.

Lu was attending to a sleep that eluded him. Had *long* eluded him. Fragments of meaning flicked in the darkness. Dreams of mindless malice walked like clay monsters in nightmares that were just dreams packed to the brim with reality.

The reality of the Survivors' new world.

Tossed and tossing still, Lu found little sleep. Bodies unfolded behind his eyes, the memory of the last moments, the end, playing and replaying over and over. He saw the uncurling lace of viscera. The red. The nakedness of humanity's lust still strong and bare-assed in the ruins of the wreckage. Gnarled steel protruding from the rubble like cracked bones, the rust licked clean by the force of the Event, the sudden blast. Bricks strewn like thrown mortar and footpaths churned into washed, gravel roads. Thousands of bodies slumped in confusion. Arms twisted tight, lacing around fleshy knees. Fingers strung together, knitting bodies into a uniform rocking. Lips mumbling a stammer, something about coffee and the pastor's sermon.

It was a Sunday when it happened.

It was hell and god was there, too.

The dead, everywhere. Like alters. Bodies piled too tall to count. Some, toward the bottom, still alive and clawing their way out, trying, but suffocating noisily on human flesh and fat instead. Meat riven along bones. Skin with ligaments dried taut as rope. Curling buckskins tanned with brain, but unstretched, undrawn. Faces like boiled pork casings that slip drunkenly away, a tug tearing, a green drool dripping. The torn and torched bodies still smiling, contorted in visages of a dying naivety, the yellow palings of their teeth the only residue of their once-humanity.

Lu played it all in his sleepless mind. Images flashing on the dark walls of his room, reflecting strangely in the polyester puddles of his sweat.

He saw the charred limbs of exploded trees stretching like sinew and sagging over the black wires of Earth. Limbs devoid of any anatomical assemblage, a medley of flesh and bone puffing a paradox of fine marble statues that crackled in clumps of charred clay. Earth taking everything back. Ash whining in the wind like parched autumn leaves. Raw red mud billowing into boils and pimple-like mounds from the heat that was transforming the once-green city parks and manicured lawns into deep craters of cleft Earth. The blackened, flame-eaten bodies of a civilization once peppered by progress now strewn everywhere. Untied and torn. Some caught mid-flight, their metallic limbs still outstretched. Charred now on the ground like strange statues. A kind of haze, an unholy mist taking everything back, ripping Earth minerals free.

Then, the runneling of flesh. Human flesh still steaming like tattered flags whirling the gloom of defeat. Putrid and swelling with puss. Tears of blood dripping from flapping meat. Flesh dangling from bones still moving, bones lacking the covering of skin and trying to get away, trying to run and find safety. But finding only hell. Only white blades of cracked bone poking through pink flesh. All dripping a gelatinous marrow.

Lu saw the wet slump.

Death sliding into dust, the crimson dirt, the dead or dying caught in the bloody work of anguish, a pain courting a confusion deeper than any thought. Until the mist and other scavengers arrived to do their work, to turn the pain into smiles, the anguish into mirth. Because death feels only love for life.

Lu's mind, even now, hears the sound of the groveling grief, of sour madness, of silent screams, of complete surprise. For no one saw it coming. No one had prepared for it, though long had the wind whispered. Though long had Earth Mother shown her many signs. The cracking. The biting pains of too much growth, splitting from stretching bones. The pittering hum of endless engines, machines always on, always thumping like cold hearts, putrid petrol organs serving only one direction. Always pushing, never inhaling back. A life of arteries. A body devoid of veins—

But everyone felt her weight when *it* finally arrived.

In sleep or out of it, Lu cried like a forlorn child and sobbed when the images swept across his mind. Every night, they found him, the faces and the bile. Every night, his bed shook with his tidal sweat and tears. Every night, he lived and relived their end.

But it was the memory of something else that haunted him, that kept *actual* sleep from slithering its dark way through his cracked window or under his covers. Like primed and dripping fangs extending from the broad head of the god killer. The image of something so simple and common that it blanched his mind forever. Past the piled corpses and leaky liquids meandering in thick, crimson streams along the boundless horizons of screaming black ruins of buildings and bodies, Lu saw something that should not have been there, but was there, and in being there, horrified him, forever.

Shoes.

Tiny, little shoes. Just a pair, yeah.

Just two small and sparkling white shoes untouched by fire and smoke. Neglected by death and unwanted by her arching tendrils, the force that came from nowhere and everywhere all at once.

But not for *them*. The shoes were perfect.

Even now, lost in the liminal between sleep and slumber, Lu remembered crawling over to them, the creamy asphalt burning his hands, the cold, grey ash puffing around him with his every strike and pull of his palms. He remembered feeling like he shouldn't. Some deep voice inside his gut telling him to stay away, to forget this place, to find survivors, to help those who made it. But he didn't listen, he couldn't listen. A mighty gravity, their story, these little shoes, pulled him into their orbit.

He crawled closer. When he saw the truth, he vomited.

It was not the shoes.

What they contained—

This was the part when he fell apart. Not because there was some glitch in the ether. Not because he was *not* suppose to fall apart.

No! No! No!

No—Lu fell apart because he was *still* alive, and to be alive is to be created to fall apart.

Laying there on the melting road, a face before the shoes, Lu curled and clutched his stomach as a heat pushed against his throat and he vomited for many minutes until only tears and tearing heaves remained. He shook and shivered. Screaming, shivering still.

What he saw, changed him forever.

There, astride the liquidous bile and hate; there, planted like two young saplings; there, untouched and perfectly pure, were two little white shoes with bright red glitter throwing back whatever sunlight was left. Sparkling and holding the light in little, glimmering motions. No child. No feet. No socks. No char. No ash. No blemish. No scuff. Just a pair of empty shoes, tightly tied with the most perfect bunny ears he ever saw. Tied and ready for running, for playing.

For playing, yeah.

How could he ever go home? Truly home? How could he ever rest? The silence was too loud. He saw them continually. Even now, in his bed, Lu saw them when he closed his eyes to sleep. They were there, always just there, in front of him. What lay behind rescripted the places that came next. The past now a future too fucked to run from, to escape. Even now. Even now.

Shoes with little white strings stretching halfway to the infinite. You had to be there. There's nothing to conceive. Empathy isn't enough, it's never enough in times like these.

Sometimes, what the world needs most is to feel for itself.

It was just a nightmare. *Just* a nightmare. The past visiting in visions, playing over and over so often that it had grown into a foul mess of composting hate in Lu's chest, the pixelated threads and glittering reds becoming strange faces sewn together and tight with strands of sinew. Contorted images shaped in heat and transformed under the glop of rot into something uniform and stable. A humus of horror turning and tumbling in his mind. His black and drowning mind. They were a plague of pattern infecting his every night's sleep.

But Lu could never create a true black. Even with his eyes closed. Was grey and punched by little pecks of glittering pinks and dancing creams, like lamb's milk frothy and boiling over a fire. Even now when he turned everything over, examining it in the dark, the loamy soil releasing its particles and all those tangy bits into the air, other colors remained. There was the black. True. And there was also the specks of red and white, the endless pink petals below fields that his visions couldn't pin down. Couldn't understand, not really. Not yet. It was a mirage of memory—the shoes, the unmoved soles, their perfectly tied white laces—living in sharp screams. Soundless screams. And muffled. Tendrils reaching from the dark, where the black grows and grows, but is never true enough to be anything else than a nightmare, a toothless dream.

When Lu woke, the rain was lashing against his window and the soggy din of the storm reminded him that his bed was wet and his bladder was full. He needed to piss.

He forced open his eyes and saw that the room was lit by the wan of a light in the hall. A nightlight, yellowing in time. Waning in age. It threw a thin ray of warm light from its little bag into the room, spilling it sloppily, the small crack in the door supplying a trace to follow. A beckoning beam, or maybe an admonishing aura, issuing warnings more like a lighthouse than an old nightlight.

But Lu's bladder couldn't wait.

He threw off the sheet in a weak manner, arms pendulating like a rotten mast below wind-beaten sails. His body hurt. His core was over-worked, straining still. Tired from trying to keep up, to perform the full work of his bottom half, his broken hull leaking water. Sinking. But the sheets splashed to the side, landing in the mere of piss or sweat beside him, and he felt naked and cold. His stiff, grey Suit glued to his frame, and rancid. Smelly.

His crawl to the bathroom was quiet and well-practiced. From birth his hips never really worked right. Life pulled strongly on them, deforming their joints, and eventually their mangled bones grew weakly and bent. Something about genetics—

His legs did not work, not anymore. And Lu often wondered why the gods gave him such worthless souvenirs.

Crawling as a cripple was one thing, but why did they have to give him a tail, a worthless rudder lugging behind? Wiggling endless trails into the oak floorboards, moving hands-first like a snail on dry ground, like a snail leaving lusty liquid smears behind, Lu smelled their sneers. His calloused hands belied his thin, weak look. The gods not only cursed him to crawl, but laughed at him and made him deal with the weight and daily reminder of his leg's dolor.

There are animals, he knew of, heard of when he was a child, who release broken appendages when they are done with them, they just let them go and move on, seemingly able to forget the whole damn thing. They have that ability. So why was he cursed to behold his own? Why was his pain prostrate before him, just there, every day of his life? When he could have just donned a torso with arms and moved on with the whole fucking affair...

It was these thoughts that challenged for that space in his mind, is dialing back the nightmare's waves to surf his own. Reality ripping, ripping.

The nightlight's rays in the hall razed the dark in tiny claps aswarm with waving maggots chewing the light that seemed to digest the dark with a steady abandon. Save for the rain bleating now on the many metal roofs of the Hamlet, Lu's movement was met with silence, a stillness as quiet as dirt atop ancient graves.

He crawled down the hallway, his legs swaying behind him. Hand, elbow—PULL. Elbow—PUSH. Hand, elbow—PULL. Drop—REST. Hand, elbow—PULL. Elbow—PUSH. Hand—

Passing his son's room. It was quiet. The door open just enough to let in a hope of light, a touch in the dark. Lu paused if only in his mind to take in the gentle patter of the boy's breathing. Measuring it against his own. It was labored and strained, though soft, like boyhood cheeks before the poke of stubble settles and plants itself firmly, forever. He listened instinctively, hearing each breath like words, breaths swelling into sentences, stories where he only remembered the best part.

Soon, Lu was in the bathroom. It was numerical, his precision. His movement was a frequent lament. Morale for him rarely lay in the numbers, the iambic meter of his strained mobility. Lu didn't take it for granted, just didn't see the point in worshiping it. Instead, he made dread a poetry. Motion, a rising meter of accented syllables burgeoning into rhyme became a blooming of horrid flowers. He welcomed the dread, the verse of loathing, because it reminded him that even something broken could have a use. That nothing is wasted. That beauty and dread are just tangled threads be-dreaming the world. Glittering or gloaming, it didn't matter. And that what is broken may in fact be what is whole in a broken world.

The bathroom's tile floor was cold beneath his hands. Colder under his wet clothes. His piss soaked Suit. Or was it sweat? He didn't care. There were presently other pressures more important, like much more important. He unwrapped the Suit from his groin, moving quickly, unbuttoning a special compartment that Salience's Department of Clothing and Bodily Comportment (The DCBC as it was called) had made just for him, and released the contents of his bladder with a blissful sigh.

The toilet was nothing special. A hole in the floor, really. The white, porcelain throne removed long ago, leaving behind a shadow of shit as an oval outline. A black stain lingering to tell of generations of faulty potty trainings. Today, only a certain flap that let certain things down and prevented certain things from coming back up resided for him to reach.

Laying on his side, arching his back, Lu let the piss go and smiled, shivering in the chill aftermath. He breathed deeply and slow. Wiggled dry, smiling.

Then, after a short collection of more breaths, he pulled himself to the sink, which was little more than a plumbed bowl on the floor. Ran the hot water. The pipes babbled strangely as they began to flow and issued a shuttering language of preternatural noise that echoed off the tiles of the room. But Lu thought nothing of it, either because he was still half-asleep, or because his mental faculties were otherwise occupied in considering the remedy for his sweat or piss soaked Suit. As one does when they find themselves soaked laying on the bathroom floor in the middle of the night...

He washed his hands. Then, he lapped the faucet's gentle stream with his lips. Feeling the water climb from cool to warm and wave over them in clean motion. Sweeping him away, pulling, tugging him to somewhere else. Somewhere so far off, and clean. A refreshing riptide. He let his tongue taste it, the fresh water, and he felt the sweat leave his face. The fresh water winning, the salt leaving, slowly, slowly, slow. Inhaling a breath, the sharp air tickling his cool throat. Laying on the floor, he breathed again and took it all in: the cataclysmic end, the bodies, the shoes, the endless nightmares, his soaked sheets, Salience's grey Suit pressing his liquids back into himself, his son's labored breathing just down the hall, the emptiness, the black.

In that moment, in the calm, Lu had not realized that he left the tap going, the faucet still singing strangely over his hands. A shock of lightless thunder ricocheted through his body when the water climbed from warm to hot to nearly boiling. Lu shot back, nerves roiling in the pain that rolled his body in a quick retreat to the opposite wall. Tucking his hands into his chest, a burn response.

But the noise in the pipes grew and the water grew and pullulated louder and louder until Lu realized that he could feel movement in the floor, some sacred dirge of demons chanting gutturally. Slithering slowly. Some song waking the deep, far below, walking, something other than water inside the old, copper pipes:

Memónha tóm
Hióm Dégom beret

Even then, half-awake, cowering in the corner, his body twisted tight from the horror, the words meant to him. A scent of clarity working through his senses like a soft hand on a tired back, or like a cool drink bittered by a citrus wedge under some distant and warm sun. But it *was* distant, the words, but they were also warm and known, like he had heard them before. A long, long time ago. In ages past. They were familiar and satisfied a deep itch in his mind, some occulation removed that let the light in. *Their* light. It sparked something in him, something deep, some cadence he had not heard in many years.

Again, the chanting gurgle from the open drain:

Memónha tóm
Hióm Dégom beret

Lu shook it off to a lack of sleep or the late night hour or some other very material problem with the architecture of the old house. But there came another sound, rising this time not from the floor-sink but the floor-toilet's flapping gullet. It pulled him back, the horror's claws and drunk his mind's tepid waters.

Lu rolled and fought even further as the horror crept jaggedly down his spine. His mind found purchase upon the pipe's chant and the bathroom began to twist and shrink in a confusion of matter. The song, again, but now in a new tongue.

I remember him.
He whom Earth bore.

The chanting and its song and the guttural clanking in all the pipes grew louder and louder, shaking and singing as it came. The languages colliding into a confluence of pure chaos, is muddy slurries of soppy spring waters drowning those who dare to walk by, or crawl...

A chug or shudder that seemed to be running through the pipes like a mouse then shot from the toilet's flap-hole and erupted a gruel of brown, brackish fluids. Chunks and heaps of tangled hair laced the terror's tail as the watery goop shot for the ceiling, nearly touching before turning and splashing upon the bathroom's white tiles, and Lu.

Lu looked up. Shouldn't have. Wet rivers ran from the corners of his eyes and disappeared into the thick grey mist of his beard. Lumps of excrement, seasoned with fresh sprinkles of piss, littered the space in a hysteria of horror. Lu gagged violently. He vomited. Heaving a spectral of bile before meal after meal followed in faucety-fashion. Barely capable of moving. Vomiting again. It filled his Suit. And so he rolled and tried to crawl away, to get out. But slipped instead, smashing his chin and chest against the once-cold tiles. The tiles that were now warm. Tiles that were brown. And slushy.

It was a smell Lu was familiar with, and his mind struggled to see through anything but a lens of memory. Before him, the Cataclysm. Piles of bodies crawling above a workforce of worms, black beetles issuing from each socket after a sumptuous dinner of innocent blue-green eyes, ravens circling and waiting to tear and nibble the fallen in their trenches, where the dead lay in corruption, their skins barely capable of concealing the maggoty motion they were now homes to.

Lu struggled to the floor-sink and twisted the metal knobs in both directions, hoping some magik or chance would cut the trick off at its source. To stop the chanting, the words. The words! The WORDS!

But there was so much more to the moment than a fault in the pipe's mechanisms, and the shit poured even higher and faster. Lu worked it all closed but the ghoulish waters only grew and grew. Streaming now. His strength matched muscle to muscle by something else—someone else? Great torrents laced the room in a mayhem so complete that Lu began to wonder if he would drown. His mind he sent above it, walking on water, and he began to craft tomorrow's headline for the paper: CRIPPLE EATS SHIT, AND DIES, or, CRIPPLE TOO TIRED TO FLUSH DIES IN PIPE MISHAP, or something fucked up like that. Yeah.

"Mishap," he said to himself through very very tight lips, thinking how that one word so aptly summed up both *this* moment and *all* other moments that had come before. "A mishap of evolution, a derelict adaption that should have terminated generations ago," Lu muttered, his mouth playing with the last part like an old man's tongue.

As though smiling thinly at his words, the chaos becomes still and calm for a white moment. Just a breath.

Trying to maintain a modicum of composure. Lu centering his mind on the peace laying under the sacredness of defeat. Speaking to the cavorting mirage of form, saying he was good with it, good with the cracking lot of it. Admitting in its ear, wherever such an organ would dwell on a hairy-fountain of human sludge, that he had long wanted someone to talk to, to make words with. It was a sentiment the horror seemed to understand, a reciprocity which urged it on.

It replied with a derisive grunt. A guttural growl.

Lu glanced back at the toilet, puttering now like a late-autumn fountain spurting a rhapsody of putrid, brown porridge over brimming bowls from the teeny-weeny at the peak all the way to the plump and great pool at the bottom. The great string of human hair that appeared from the flap-hole had now risen up to the surface of the floor's broad bowl in several places and were weaving themselves together, forming what was unmistakably a mat. The jaunty and clumpy liquids gyring like a whirl of fish or a skirl of heavy fumes caught in the mat's tight weave.

Lu looked at the bizarre tapestry and marveled at its perfection. If it would have been anything other than human hair encaging human shit and colored by human piss, it would have been beautiful...

Out of the morass of human filth expanded a nothing so heavy that it nearly shattered the film of scuffed dust that had scuttled into the corners of the ceiling and floor alike with preternatural abandon. The dirt that was running away. Screaming. Levitating or leaving in fear of becoming *actually* filthy.

Lu was entranced. Even then, was enraptured by the gruesome reality, the fact that *this* horror was just *his* body's processes thrown back at him in no less kind of a manner than he threw it down to begin with. Pipes taking and pipes giving. It made him sick. It sucked whatever energy he had left and drained his mind of all other thoughts. He lay there, lost and covered in filth, nearly drowning at the fountain of forgotten waste.

It ate at Lu's gut and he considered the *source*. Why such thoughts came to him in that moment, he never did know.

For he was interrupted by something else. Something even more sinister, like long nails from curling claws rasping the wood of the front door, or like a woman's thighs spreading and there finding only a mare's muzzle. Just then another force joined the clanking pipes and the chanting songs and the rasping wood. It didn't come from the floor or the pipes or the infinite outside laying beyond the walls. No, it came from down the hall. Lu was sure of it. It sounded eerily like a child's scream. A thin wail snuffed out and early by hands or a hailing hell.

It sounded close. Like really close. Like his son was just there in the room with him. With him and also somewhere else, somewhere very distant. Lu was in shock. He scanned the room with his eyes and watched the paint peel and flicker like blown candle flames. His nerves jumped from his body to the room and from the room his heart soared into new elevations. He pawed at the floor and screamed from the bathroom in leaps.

What he saw next, changed everything.

It was when he *really* fell apart...

"There's no way," he said. "I am dreaming." Lu started digging up what he needed to tell himself. Excavating excuses. Telling himself the lies he knew weren't true. That this is just a dream, or saying something like that. Because ghosts need anchors too, roots in the physical world, don't they? But his heart knew better and screamed and his voiced followed, matching the weight with an energy all of his own, throwing air from his lungs whose power now felt alien to him. He screamed and fought forward as though a burning pan laced his bare hands. The sound of searing flesh. Of boiling skin. He shook to wake himself. He tore at his skin, sending nerves like picks to prick his eyes to open. To dig at the ice, the stupor, the putrid pallor of be-dreaming horror.

But he didn't wake, for he wasn't dreaming.